MW00779202

PRETTY SHATTERED SOUL

ROBBI RENEE

SYNOPSIS

Trauma left her captivating, sweet soul flawed, distressed, disconnected, and shattered. Savvy and effortlessly beautiful, Syncere James concealed her heartache, finding security and refuge in her career as a successful real estate agent. Refusing to lose control, Syncere dictates and schedules every aspect of her life, including her relationships with men. The pretty princess never desired the love of a prince, then she met a King.

Wealthy construction company owner, King Cartwright, could have the heart of any woman in Haven Point, but he only has eyes for the gorgeous and complicated Syncere James. Navigating her complex layers, will his persistence and protection win her love? Or are Syncere's unreasonable barriers and immeasurable pain too much for King to make her his queen?

DEDICATION
MY LIFE'S TRINITY - GRACE. GRIND. GRATITUDE.

Dedicated to my wonderfully amazing and patient husband. Your love notes have been my daily inspiration to love with grace, stay on my grind, and always be grateful. I love you always!

#bae #MEB #gerty #sasha #ilovemesomehim

LOVE NOTES
BY ROBBI RENEE

PROLOGUE

"Syncere, I can't believe you are going out with Davis. Girl, *the* Davis Dubois. You do realize his family has a building on campus named after them. Like a whole ass building, Prima." Syncere's cousin and college roommate Symphony, or *Prima 'Pri'* as they referred to one another, squealed. "What are you going to wear?" Symphony questioned, sifting through the miniature closet in the corner of their powder-blue painted dorm room.

"We're just going to see *Welcome Home Roscoe Jenkins* and maybe grab some food, so something casual should be fine." Syncere shrugged. She never really stressed over her appearance or attire, probably because Syncere James' ravishing, hourglass figure would look good in a trash bag. Syncere was pretty, mysteriously gorgeous - glowing mahogany skin, the most unusual greyish brown almond-shaped eyes, leading to her delicately curved nose and plump, pouty, silken Meagan Good-*ish* lips.

She was in her junior year at Monroe University. Syncere was highly intelligent and popular - full academic scholarship, student government secretary, and chapter treasurer of her sorority. Her latest claim to fame was being pursued by one of the finest men on campus, Davis Dubois. Davis was a senior star basketball athlete majoring in political science. His family was Monroe University royalty. His father, Reed Dubois, MBA, J.D., dean of the business school, and his mother, Dr. Priscilla Dubois, an award-winning author, and esteemed psychology professor.

After graduation, Davis was headed to Howard University Law School on a full scholarship. He was perfect and Syncere was smitten. While most girls would lay their panties at his feet, Syncere was not really tripping off of Davis - ignoring his advances until he left roses and candy in front of her dorm room. Although she was playing hard to get, she wasn't blind. Davis was fine - thickset, bubbling brown sugar, cock diesel kinda fine. And *he* wanted *her*.

"Prima, this is Davis we're talking about. You already know he's going to be fly as hell, so your ass *will not* wear some plain old jeans and t-shirt." Symphony's voice was muffled while buried in the closet, continuing to shuffle for the perfect outfit. "Here, wear this. It's sexy, but just enough material to keep him intrigued - and guessing." Symphony smacked her lips as if it sealed the deal for Syncere.

"Prima, you want me to put all this James' family DNA ass in these little shorts?" Syncere held the shorts up to the light, attempting to locate the rest of the material. "And these tall ass wedge heels - really?" She paused, shaking her head in concern. "Pri, I don't know about this."

"Heffa, that's why I picked the flowy shirt, duh." Symphony rolled her eyes. "Like I said, just enough skin to keep him interested. You gotta keep a nigga like double D on his toes." The cousins howled, falling back onto one of the twin beds.

———————

DAVIS PULLED up to the front of Betty Shabazz Hall in a midnight blue, sparkling clean Jeep Grand Cherokee. Syncere immediately noticed his pristine Retro Carolina Blue Jordan's casing his gigantic feet. Brawny thighs gratifying his plaid Polo shorts, exposing Hershey kiss-shaped and colored calves. Complimentary crisp white V-neck Polo t-shirt pleasantly crowded by his muscular frame. A diamond-encrusted #33 charm dangling from his gold chain, glistened against his expansive nape, leading to the most beautifully crafted lips and honey-brown orbs that glistened when he eyed her.

"Well, hello sweetness." Syncere shuddered at Davis's thunderous deep-toned voice. "You look tasty enough to eat." His 6'2" frame perfectly paired with her five-foot, seven-inch physique as he planted a tender forehead kiss.

"Hi, Davis." Syncere battled with the squeal that brewed in her larynx. "I see you flaunting your baller status as usual."

The women of Shabazz Hall crowded the lobby and dorm room windows as Davis and Syncere departed. Her dorm mates were pissed. Yearning - shit, lusting to be the lucky lady cradling Davis' athletic limbs tonight.

The cute couple heartily laughed through Martin Lawrence's latest box office hit. Sharing tender exchanges as their hands connected in the extra-large bucket of buttered popcorn. Davis wrapped one husky arm around Syncere's shoulders while he clutched the available hand in his. Syncere was beaming.

They dined at a local pub, popular among Monroe University students. All eyes were on Davis and Syncere with agreeable sentiments that they could be a power couple on campus. Sharing buffalo wings and chicken quesadillas, over a Jack and Coke for him and a Malibu Rum and pineapple juice for her, they chatted aimlessly about their present and future.

Noticing Syncere's glass was empty, Davis uttered, "You can have another drink if you want it, sweetness." He winked.

"Nah, I'm good. One is my limit. Besides, I have to work tomorrow." Syncere shrugged.

"You work at the writing center right?" Davis paused.

"Yeah. Gotta keep my scholarship, so twelve hours a week at the writing center it is."

"That's what's up. You gotta do what you gotta do." He nodded.

"Most definitely. My grandparents can't afford for me to lose my scholarship so I stay focused on grades and work. But it's almost over for you. I heard you got accepted into Howard Law School. That's what's up." Seated close to him in the half-circle shaped booth, she nudged her elbow against his arm.

4

"Thank you beautiful. I appreciate that." He leaned in, breathing against her cheek before sharing those perfectly crafted lips.

The blaring screech of Davis's phone interrupted his invasion of her cheek.

"Hello. What's up Q? You locked out? Damn man, right now? Aight dawg. I got you." Syncere deciphered the cryptic conversation and assumed their date would be concluded as soon as Davis disconnected the call.

"Is everything ok?" Syncere questioned, secretly hoping that whoever that was didn't need Davis' assistance at that moment.

Davis sighed. "My roommate Quincy lost his keys at the gym. Coach has him on curfew because of his grades so he needs to get in our apartment so he can check-in before curfew." Stroking the curve of her face, he whispered, "I'm sorry sweetness, but I need to go. I'll swing by my apartment then take you home."

Driving up to his apartment that was less than ten minutes from campus, Quincy was in fact sitting on the steps leading up to their second-floor apartment.

"I really don't want you to sit in the car alone. Can you come in?" Davis requested.

"I thought you just needed to give him the key?" She curiously inquired.

"I do. But I gotta take a piss." He fixed his hand across his crotch.

Syncere chuckled. "Yeah, I do too. I guess the blueberry slush, water, and alcohol caught up with us."

Davis exited the truck, jogging to the passenger side to gather Syncere.

"Q, this is Syncere. Syncere, my boy Quincy." Davis kept moving up the steps towards the apartment as he spoke. Syncere smiled, and Quincy nodded, solidifying their introduction, although they'd seen each other around campus and at basketball games.

Surprisingly, the apartment was neatly kept for two gigantic basketball players. The bedrooms were positioned on each end of the apartment with the living area and kitchen in the middle. Davis's room had an ensuite bathroom while Quincy's was shared with guests.

"Can I use this bathroom?" Syncere pointed towards the guest bathroom door.

"Sweetness, you don't want to use Q's bathroom," Davis whispered while turning up his nose. He mouthed, "that shit is nasty." Syncere chuckled as Davis led her to his bathroom.

Syncere exited the bathroom, glancing around Davis's meticulously kept room, still drying her hands with a paper towel. Davis was perched against the headboard of the bed, focused on his phone.

"Hey." She whispered, pulling him from his daze.

"Hey, you. Come here for a second." He curved his pointer finger, beckoning her to him.

"What's up?" Syncere cautiously proceeded, standing at the end of the bed. Patting the pockets of her shrunken shorts, she realized her purse and phone were in the car.

"I thought we could just chill for a little bit." Davis bit the corner of his lip, looking sexy and dangerous. A bubble of intuition started to simmer in her gut. Syncere continued to observe the room - his door was closed and apparently locked as evidenced by the keyed deadbolt on the bedroom door. *Who the fuck has a deadbolt on their bedroom door?* The simmering intuitiveness quickly escalated to a full volcanic eruption. Syncere was nervous, uneasy, afraid.

"I wish I could, but I really need to get home, Davis. Remember, I have to work tomorrow? And I left my phone in the car. I'm sure my cousin has called me." She tensely blushed, footing across the brown carpet towards the door, confirming that it was locked.

Davis stood from the bed, hands stuffed in his plaid pockets, an indecent grin plastered across his diminishing dapper features. His height monumentally more intimidating than it appeared earlier.

"I'm not ready for you to go home, Syncere." His aesthetically pleasing brown eyes were now perilously darkened, apathetic - horrifying.

"Davis, um, can you just unlock the door and take me home? I - I'm ready to go back to my dorm." She stuttered with her back to the door, futilely turning the knob. Syncere x-rayed the room, searching for any form of protection or escape.

"Syncere, you came over here with those little ass shorts on, looking so fucking good, and now you want to go home?" Davis heavily pressed against her frame, breath fogging the whites of her eyes. "Like I said. I ain't ready to take your fine ass home beautiful. Besides, I'm Davis Dubois baby - what I want, I get."

"Davis, you're scaring me." Syncere quaked as a single tear stained her face. "Just unlock the door and let me get my purse, please." She was eerily placid, still breathless. "Davis, I'll walk home. Just please let me go."

The still approach was not working as Davis continued to abbreviate the already minimal distance between them, firmly grabbing her face, forcing his tongue through her tightly sealed lips. Syncere bit his tongue and yelled, "Quincy, please help me!" Banging on the door, the wall, Syncere clamored, screaming and hollering - praying for a lifeline.

"Ouch! Shit! This bitch bit me." The anger in Davis' eyes was blood red.

"Help! Davis, please don't do this." She pleaded.

"Shut up Sweetness! What the fuck is wrong with you? You've been playing games with me for weeks, teasing me this whole time." Davis snatched the distressed cries from her lips with a blistering strike across her pretty terrorized face.

Syncere desperately fought to get away. Scratching, kicking, shouting - pondering, *where the fuck is Quincy?* She was prepared to leap from the second-floor window if she had to. *I would rather die.*

"Bring your ass back here, beautiful!" Davis continued his petrifying gentlemanly banter, uttering *beautiful and sweetness* while feloniously battering her wounded treasure.

"Davis! No. Please stop. You're hurting me. Oh God, please help me. I can't breathe. Please, don't do this. Davis. No!"

1

Panting, heaving, labored breathing, drenched in sweat, eyes dilated - practically hyperventilating, Syncere awakened from the unrelenting nightmare she'd periodically endured for the past ten years. As the days expired leading to the anniversary of that traumatic night, it vividly looped repeatedly in her head. The lucid nightmares felt so real that Syncere frantically reached for her face, tasting remnants of blood on her tongue, caressing the hallucinated sting of being slapped and choked.

Although the result of that dreadful night remained the same, Syncere constantly reprimanded herself for the decisions leading up to the damaging incident - questioning could she have done more to stop him. *Maybe I shouldn't have worn those shorts? I should've just stayed in the car.* With every restless night's slumber, her mind, body, and soul painstakingly revived the harm. Ten years had vanished, the agonizing memories temporarily buried deep, locked away in an unattainable vault. But last night, and a few nights prior, the gnawing retrospection was ever-present.

"Stop this shit Syncere! You didn't do anything wrong." Syncere battled with herself for several moments before the blaring ring of the cell phone pulled her from self-destruction.

"Hey, Prima." Syncere greeted Symphony without looking at the phone since her cousin acted as her personal alarm clock almost every morning- not at Syncere's request. At only 11 months older, Symphony thought she was Syncere's protector. The cousins were often mistaken for sisters because of their twin orbs and hips, but they were definitely best friends. Syncere and Symphony were raised by their grandparents because both of their mothers didn't really take the job as *mom* very seriously.

"Hey, Prima. You up boo?" Symphony questioned.

"Yes, Pri. I've been up. Up too damn early actually."

"Are you feeling ok?" Symphony inquired, sensing something strange about her cousin's tone.

"Mmmhmm, I'm fine." Syncere's default response was always *I'm fine* when she was far from it.

"It happened again didn't it?" Silence invaded the phone. "Prima?" Symphony's voice elevated. "Syncere, answer me. You had the nightmare again didn't you?"

The sound of Syncere's tears responded before her words. "Yes Symphony, but I'm fine. I'll get past it, just like I always do."

"Pri, this has been happening off and on for weeks. And it always happens before the anniversary of when everything happened."

"Anniversary?" Syncere shouted. "That makes it sound celebratory and there *ain't shit* to celebrate about that day." Her intonation remained escalated.

"You know I didn't mean it like that Pri." Symphony paused, choosing her next words carefully, attempting to avoid further tongue-lashing. "Maybe it's time for you to go back to Dr. Jacky. Talking to her helped the last time, remember."

Do I remember? What kind of question is that? How the hell could I forget the years of therapy. She mused, still annoyed by her cousin's interrogation.

"Symphony, I'm-"

"*Fine*. Yeah, I know." Symphony angrily interjected. "But keep going with that response if you want to when I know damn well you *ain't* fine. You know I'll always be here when you're ready to talk."

"Just let it go Pri. I don't need you to Iyanla me today. I need to get ready for work anyway." Syncere desperately wanted to change the subject, otherwise, Symphony would attempt to fix Syncere's life with all of her Iyanla-isms.

"Heffa, your apartment is in the same building as your office. It takes two minutes to walk down the steps. And it's Friday anyway. You can work from home so what the hell you gotta get ready for?" Symphony paused while Syncere remained tongueless, not desiring to disclose her reason for going into the office.

"Oh, I know. You trying to get cute for Lion King?" Symphony squealed, dragging out the words which irritated her cousin.

"Bye Symphony Monique James!" Syncere squawked as she laughed.

"But you know I'm right. Bye Syncere Monae James!"

SYMPHONY WAS correct about at least one thing- Syncere did in fact live in the same building that housed the office of Davenport Realty, where she was the top sales agent and marketing manager for the past five years. But her desire to go into the office had nothing to do with *him*, at least that's what she told herself.

The ceramic tile floor was cool to Syncere's French manicured feet as she padded across the bathroom to turn on the shower. While the multi-jet shower began to steam, she removed her tank top and boy shorts that were soaked and sticky with sweat. Glaring in the lightly fogged full-length mirror hanging from the linen closet, Syncere examined her frame - full breasts, taut waist, immaculately curvy hips, and ample thighs. Running her fingers through her summertime Senegalese twist that protected her natural coils, she stretched, gazing at the faded curved scar just below her navel that was covered by an infinity symbol tattoo with the word *survivor* inscribed.

Syncere was exhausted, yawning and stretching to loosen her limbs. But the weariness and fatigue were camouflaged by her natural beauty. Syncere was mesmeric - effortlessly gorgeous, but her devastating past rendered her severely scorned - broken.

Syncere carefully stepped into the steamy shower, soaking every inch of her curvy body with vanilla shea butter scrub. Allowing the jets to joyfully massage her frame, Syncere let the water stream down her face, erasing remnants of dried tears and restlessness. The steam shower served a greater purpose, extracting the literal and figurative toxins that invaded her anatomy.

Stepping out of the shower, she seriously contemplated staying in bed all day, wearing nothing but her robe. Syncere was long overdue for a mental health day filled with mindless reality TV and strawberry cheesecake ice cream.

Draped in a plush white robe, she footed out of her bedroom into the modern kitchen designed with white granite countertops, black cabinetry with shiny chrome hardware, and turned on the kettle to heat water for her peppermint tea. It seemed to help put her in a better mood after a night of horrid recollection.

Blowing to cool the steamy tea, Syncere journeyed back to her bedroom into the perfectly organized closet. Sifting through the rows of summer skirts and dresses, Syncere chuckled, pondering her cousin's earlier accusations. Since it was Friday, she really could've opted to work from home or to wear the Davenport Realty polo and some jeans or khakis. *I wonder if he will be in the office today.* She mused.

"Maybe Prima was right. I'm getting all dolled up just to go downstairs. Just to see *him*." She briefly debated. Pulling her braids into a high ponytail and tying down her meticulously laid edges, Syncere dressed in an eggplant color fitted t-shirt dress that fell right above the knee, gold Michael Kors sandals, and a distressed jean jacket since the office temperature stayed on arctic.

Since she didn't have any clients today, Syncere was

thankful for a fairly stress-free beautifully sunny Friday and decided she would drop by the office before heading to the neighborhood coffee shop, *The Brown Bean*. The coffee shop was one of the many booming businesses in the Haven Point neighborhood where Syncere grew up. After some tumultuous years, the neighborhood was revitalized with middle-class Black families and young professionals. Haven Point had experienced its very own renaissance. Black-owned businesses were thriving, buildings restored, and new construction condos and villas were sprouting up everywhere - which was great for Syncere's pockets. Davenport Realty cornered the market, managing sales and construction of all the new build homes in Haven Point and neighboring community Grover Heights.

2

"Hi, Ms. Ella. Happy Friday." Syncere pleasantly greeted Ella Davenport, the office manager and mother of co-owners Justin and Jeremiah Davenport.

"Happy Friday Syncere. You look pretty as always." Ms. Ella smiled.

"Thank you, ma'am. I'm going to grab some coffee, do you want anything?" Syncere questioned.

"Oh, no thank you, Sweetie. That's already been taken care of." Ms. Ella's ruby-red lips curved to a bright, yet sneaky smile, shifting her head towards the front door as the bell chimed.

Syncere was frozen. Her heart plummeted to her pretty toes. Little beads of sweat swelled on the small of her back. Feet heavy like boulders, unmovable because it was *him* - King Cartwright. King was the owner of King Construction, the exclusive construction partner for Davenport Realty. King was breathtaking.

Dark as night, with a coal-black low cut, wavy tresses, and a thick freshly cut beard to match. His obsidian eyes twinkled when he smiled, providing healing energies resembling the precious gemstone. Standing several inches over six feet, he had chiseled *everything* and massive, sizey thighs that deliciously filled his charcoal grey slacks. Syncere x-rayed the burgundy King Construction polo, envisioning being wrapped in those Herculean arms that firmly caressed his sleeves, offering a peek of his fraternity brand. You would've thought this was her first time laying eyes on the man.

King unveiled senses and desires in Syncere that she'd never experienced. He was charming, thoughtful, sexy as hell, and adorably sweet for such a gigantic, intimidating structure. While those should have been qualities Syncere required of a man, she preferred the unattached, noncommittal type of dude, yet *sexy as hell* was always a prerequisite.

"Hey, Pretty Lady." King smiled, admiring the way Syncere's curves pleasantly crowded her fitted dress. She was beautiful, but she had no words - soundless.

"Princess? Syncere? You ok?" King questioned with a furrowed brow, trying to figure out why she was staring at him like a piece of buttery fried chicken.

His bass-filled timbre brought her back to reality. "Oh, I'm sorry. Hey King. Happy Friday." She beamed, crossing her legs at the ankles to calm her quivering treasure.

"Happy Friday." He replied, extending a twin beaming smile to her. "Here you go Ms. Ella, one iced coffee and

Syncere, one Americano just like you like it." King winked, handing her the coffee cup.

"And exactly how do I like my coffee, King?" Syncere tilted her head, placing one hand on her abundant hip. She was prepared to walk down the street to get her coffee prepared correctly because she knew this wasn't going to be right.

"Large Americano, heavy whipping cream steamed, four Splendas, four Sugars in the Raw, a shot each of vanilla and caramel flavor." He rattled off unflinching, almost daring Syncere to refute.

Syncere fell mute - again. He delivered her coffee requirements almost better than she did - shit, she sometimes forgot to add the flavor shots. But how did he know that?

"Wow! Um, how do you know that?" Syncere examined the coffee cup as if it was laced with venom before she blew then took a sip. *Damn, it's perfect too.*

"Do you remember when I literally ran into you at the Brown Bean a few weeks ago spilling your coffee all over everything?" He chuckled, recalling being so enthralled with her that he became clumsy, causing her to spill the perfect Americano all over several contracts. "I heard you ordering when I was at the counter ready to pay for it." He shrugged.

"And you committed *my* coffee order to your memory?" Syncere was seriously shocked at his attention to detail while Ms. Ella's eyes and perfectly bobbed hair darted back and forth between Syncere and King, favoring the flirtatious exchange.

"Yeah, Princess. I remember everything about you." King

coyly admitted. "Oh, I almost forgot, one stuffed croissant. I copped the last one." He proudly pronounced.

Syncere loved the Asiago cheese and spinach stuffed croissant from the coffee shop, but again she wondered, why does he remember these little details about her? Like one day last week he overheard her raving about the chocolate covered pineapples she bought her grandmother from *Edible Arrangements,* a few days later, Syncere walked into her office greeted by a beautiful bouquet of chocolate-covered pineapples and strawberries. His note simply said, *For Princess, Just Because. From King.*

"Thanks, King. You didn't have to do that but I really do appreciate you." She blushed, cheeks redden from the hot coffee and King.

"Anytime Pretty Lady." He winked.

And King meant that shit. In his eyes, Syncere was *his* princess, the prettiest lady he'd ever seen, and she could have whatever she liked, at any time. He admired Syncere from afar since the first day his company solidified the contract with Davenport Realty. That was eight months ago and he'd been subtly shooting his shot ever since.

Syncere's beauty could not be denied, but King adored her spirit. She was jovial, giggly, fun-loving, but there were also moments when he sensed suffering, anguish, uncertainty. King's friend and co-owner of Davenport Realty, Justin, warned him about Syncere. Not in a bad way, but because she was delicate and layered. Justin was also protective of her, like a big brother.

. . .

"You gonna keep staring at her or ask her out again?" Justin walked out of his office into the main area where King was sitting. King was gazing at Syncere while she sat in her glass-front office, head down focused on work.

"Whatever man." King chuckled. "What's up Justin?" King extended his fist to exchange a dap.

Justin laughed. "I'm good bro. What did you bring her today? A card, candy, flowers?" He teased, referencing the fact that King was rarely empty-handed, often showering Syncere with niceties.

"Man, I brought Ms. Ella some coffee." King rebutted, avoiding eye contact.

"And Syncere too." Ms. Ella blurted out peeking around the partition behind the receptionist desk. "He remembered all of that shit she puts in her coffee." Ms. Ella giggled while Justin and King joined with a hearty laugh.

"King, bro. I told you Syn be on some other shit. She don't do relationships. The only dude I've seen her kicking it with - she says they're just friends and that seems to be true because that nigga be in these streets with hella chicks."

"So, what are you saying? I should just leave her alone?" King was irritated.

"Nah. I'm saying don't get your hopes up about a relationship with Syncere James. Like I said, relationships ain't her thing. Syn is like my sister and she's cool as hell, but I don't think she's looking for a man right now, bro." Justin patted him on the shoulder as King kept his focus on Syncere.

"Man, who said anything about a relationship? You act like I'm trying to wife her." King was trying to convince himself more than Justin.

"Dawg, the way you look at Syncere...you are *definitely* trying to make her Mrs. Cartwright. Dude, you ready to turn over the family fortune for a piece of Syncere James." Justin chortled.

"Nah, I'm just hella intrigued," King uttered, narrowing his eyes and peering at Syncere.

"Whatever you say, man." Justin wasn't convinced. "Just be careful with her dawg. I don't know what it is, but Syncere has been through some shit, man."

Still eavesdropping, Ms. Ella chimed into the conversation. "It's going to take time, patience, and an act of God to knock down that girl's protective barriers."

"I hear you, Ms. Ella. I got the time and patience - but I may need one of your twenty minute alter prayers to solicit an act of God." King guffawed.

"You ready to go make this money?" Justin interrupted. They dapped in agreement before walking into Justin's office for their meeting.

King desired more from Syncere, he craved her. Not sexually, although he was consistently quieting the thundering roar of his growing erection in her presence. Syncere was mysterious - authoritative and strong-willed in her business dealings, yet eluding and apprehensive anytime he endeavored to pursue her further. King was desperate to get into that pretty little head of hers, but he would take Justin's advice and Ms. Ella's prayers.

After leaving his meeting, he couldn't help himself. He just had to lay eyes on her one more time before leaving the office, so he made his way to her office.

"Knock, knock." King rapped on Syncere's cracked office door before he entered. "Is it ok if I come in?"

"Hey. Yes. Come in. I didn't know you were still here. What can I do for you?" She gazed over the red-rimmed glasses, delightful eyes staring back at him.

Syncere was trying to play it cool, but King made her damn palms sweat and her treasure throb. *This mutherfucker is fine. Damn!* Syncere adjusted in her office chair trying to calm the commotion happening between her thighs.

"Two questions for you." He paused. "Did your client finalize their floor plan for the villa in Grover Heights? We need to order the materials."

"Which client? I have two contracts for Grover Heights." Syncere proudly stated.

"Oh, look at you superstar. I guess you can take off the rest of the month. Hitting quotas early and shit." King joked.

"Try *exceeding* quotas early and shit." She squealed as they laughed.

Glancing at his iPad, King responded. "The Smith contract."

"Yep. I have it right here. Mr. Smith emailed this morning and they are going with the Palomar floor plan." She confirmed.

"Good choice. I'll get the order started then." King paused much longer than intended, admiring how the red glasses accentuated those gorgeous grey orbs.

"King? You said you had two questions." Syncere interrupted his daze.

"Oh, yeah. Um, what are you up to this weekend?"

"Nothing really. Girls night with my cousin tonight. I have a few clients tomorrow afternoon. Why?"

They were interrupted by Ms. Ella's voice coming through the phone speaker. "Syncere, you have a visitor."

She instructed Ms. Ella to send the visitor back to her office without inquiring about who it was. Syncere figured it was a client until—

"What's up baby girl? Have you had lunch yet? I thought we could head upstairs and—" Lamont paused once he saw mountainous ass King standing in the corner. Syncere tried not to roll her eyes, frustrated by Lamont's untimely interruption. Lamont was Syncere's current noncommitted arrangement off and on for the past year. He was good for a fun outing, great sex, and no obligation - just like Syncere preferred. Lamont stopping by for a *lunch date* in her apartment wasn't an unusual request - shit, typically a welcomed inquiry. But today, it was just hella inconvenient.

"Hi, Lamont. I didn't know you were in town. I'm actually heading out early so I'll be skipping lunch today." She gave him a *what the fuck are you doing here* look, peering between him and King. "Oh, I didn't mean to be rude. Lamont Burris, this is King Cartwright... King, Lamont." They exchanged dry greetings.

"Princess, I'll let you get back to it. Have a good weekend." King was visibly irritated at the sight of Lamont. And King knew exactly what Lamont was referring to for lunch in her apartment. *So, is this her man or her fuckboy?* King pondered and was pissed.

SYNCERE LEFT the office a few hours early, not to have lunch with Lamont, but to run some errands, get her nails done, and meet Symphony for girls' night which started at Oak Grove Assisted Living where their grandmother resided. Mrs. Neolla James was 75 years old with beautiful silver shoulder-length wavy hair, greyish-brown almond eyes that she passed to her granddaughters, and ample hips that she once flaunted before getting ill. Neolla had suffered two strokes that left her wheelchair-bound, but she was mentally sharp as a tack.

"Hey, G-ma. Don't you look pretty today?" Syncere and Symphony said almost in unison.

"Well, it is Friday and I have to look my best for my favorite girls." Neolla gleamed with pride. "Give me kisses." She pulled each girl into an embrace. "What did you bring me today?"

The cousins spent just about every Friday afternoon with their grandmother and would always bring her favorite Friday meal - fish and spaghetti and a surprise dessert. Neolla loved sweets but was a diabetic, so her granddaughters allowed her to indulge once a week.

"Here's your fish and spaghetti from Melvin's. He said hi by the way." Symphony winked.

"Girl, ain't nobody thinking about Melvin's nasty ass." Neolla rolled her eyes.

"G-ma!" Both girls shouted with laughter.

"Ooohhh, you are a mess lady." Syncere chuckled,

handing her grandmother the surprise dessert. Syncere made the banana pudding just like G-ma taught her.

"This looks delicious. Thank you, girls." Neolla did a little shimmy in her wheelchair, moving the parts that were still functional.

Syncere and Symphony worked hard to ensure their grandmother had the best care after the last stroke. The doctors said she wouldn't walk, talk, and would have limited mobility in her arms. But after Symphony, who was a registered nurse, cursed a few doctors, researched the best diets, supplements, and physical therapy routines for a person with their grandmother's condition, Neolla had full mobility in her upper body, defying the doctors' expectations.

The cousins owed their lives to Mylon and Neolla James. Their grandparents raised them since they were five years old. Syncere's mother couldn't kick her drug and men addiction, and Symphony's mother chased her dream of being an actress but drank heavily and pretty much went crazy. Neither girl had seen their mothers in years. And their fathers - well Syncere's father died in a car accident when she was ten and Symphony's dad paid child support to Mr. and Mrs. James, but he was married with a family of his own so he'd never had a relationship with his daughter.

Neolla and her husband Mylon gained full custody of both girls and they worked their fingers to the bone to provide for their granddaughters; Neolla at the local bank and Mylon was a mailman. Neolla always blamed herself for her daughters' mischief but prayed to the heavens that her granddaughters would make better choices.

"G-ma? What are we playing today, Tunk or Spades? I'm

sure Mr. Henry will come and be our fourth." Symphony winked again.

"Don't call Henry's funky behind in here. He'll eat up all my damn fish." She blushed.

"Neolla James, you are wilding today." Syncere chortled as the three James women boisterously laughed, tears escaping their eyes.

After enjoying the early evening with their grandmother, they returned to Syncere's apartment to complete girls' night with a few bottles of Black Girl Magic rosé, music, a movie, and leftover spaghetti from Melvin's.

MELVIN'S WAS a local spot that had been around Haven Point for over 30 years; the best spot in the city for fried chicken and fish. A restaurant by day and a club at night since Mr. Melvin's son Lonnie recently started managing the historic establishment, expanding the space to include a dance floor and DJ.

"Prima, girl, why did Lamont come to my office today talking about he was hoping we could have lunch?" Syncere motioned air quotes. "I was meeting with King and here comes Lamont interrupting us - I mean - me." Syncere corrected.

"Oh, you were meeting with Lion King, huh?" Symphony fell out laughing on the couch. Syncere despised the nickname but joined in on the guffaw. "But ain't that how you and Lamont usually get down though?"

"I mean, yeah, but it was just bad timing." Syncere shrugged.

"Why? Because Lion King - I mean King was in your office. So, you trippin' off what King thinks now? Does he know about your little book of rules, Syncere?" Symphony teased.

"First of all, I don't have a rule book, they're preferences, but whatever! And second, no I'm not trippin' off of King or what King thinks."

"Bullshit!" Symphony coughed out the word.

Rolling her eyes, with her middle finger raised, Syncere continued. "I just would've preferred that Lamont called or text me first like he normally does."

"Uh oh. Lamont's about to get the boot because he broke a Syncere rule." Symphony joked. "Or maybe he's getting kicked to the curb because you like King - just admit it, Pri." She paused. "Shit, what's not to like? That nigga is fine, wealthy, and more fine. And he has big, um - feet. His Lion King ass can *mu-fuck-a* me anytime."

"Prima!" Syncere squawked at her cousin's nastiness. "Your ass is trifling as hell. You have disgraced a perfectly good family movie." The cousins were a little tipsy so their giggling was on ten.

"Let's go somewhere, Prima." Symphony blurted as she leaped from the couch, dancing to the background music. "I don't want to play hermit tonight. This is my weekend off and I want to kick it." Symphony started fluttering her eyelashes with her hands in prayer. "Please, Prima. You'll be my favorite cousin."

"Bitch, I'm your only cousin." Syncere cackled. "Pri, I don't feel like dressing up. I just want to chill. I wanna play hermit tonight." She whined, jokingly kicking her feet.

"Well let's just go to Melvin's. We can wear a damn paper bag and we'll still be the cutest bitches in there, trust."

"Symphony! Ugh!" Syncere complained.

"It's a beautiful night. We can walk down there, do a little dancing, find some fine ass dudes to buy our drinks, and then come back home. Simple." Syncere winked.

"We don't need another mutherfucking thing to drink." Syncere declared.

"No, bitch. Maybe *you* don't need another drink, but I could go for a *Major Pain.*" Symphony started twerking because that's exactly what a major pain drink from Melvin's would have her doing. Nobody, but Mr. Melvin knew what the hell was in that drink, but it knocked you on your ass, requiring the bartender to often relinquish car keys from drunk patrons.

"You do realize they make you sign a damn waiver before you drink that shit?" Syncere teased with a furrowed brow.

"Well, where do I sign because I'm about to get hella bent. Come on Prima. Please!" Symphony begged.

After an hour of bitching and complaining, Syncere found herself walking out of her front door in some cute dark-distressed skinny jeans, a white racerback tank, sheer enough to expose remnants of her shiny red bra, coordinating with her red Tory Burch sandals; braids pulled into a high bun, large silver hoops, and red Fenty lips. Syncere and Symphony locked arms to trek two blocks through the Haven Point neighborhood to Melvin's.

3

Fridays at Melvin's was 90s hip hop and R&B night and it was packed with beautifully melanated bodies. Syncere's mood shifted a bit once the sounds of some of her favorite music massaged her ears. Linked hand-in-hand, Symphony and Syncere navigated through the crowd looking for seats when Syncere spotted Lamont. She didn't really want to be bothered, but she knew Lamont had VIP access that he would happily extend to her.

"What's up baby girl? You're looking delicious as usual. You know that's one of my favorite bras, right?" Lamont caressed Syncere's waist, pulling her into a firm hug. Syncere couldn't deny his charisma and sexiness. Lamont was fine. Like Morris Chestnut in *The Best Man* kinda fine. He retired from the NFL after a career-ending injury and was now a talent scout, among other business endeavors. Lamont constantly traveled, but when he was in town, he never hesitated to connect with Syncere. They had a mutual understanding - searing, satisfying, thigh-aching sex. No more. No less.

"Shut up Lamont. I'm good. What's up with you?" She blushed.

Lamont directed his attention to Symphony who was trying to ignore him.

"Hi Symphony," Lamont shouted.

"Lamont." Symphony nastily nodded her head in acknowledgment and sashayed away.

Symphony didn't like the arrangement between Syncere and Lamont. She desired love, marriage, and babies for her cousin, and Lamont was not the one to give Syncere any of those things.

"Y'all so damn petty." Syncere chuckled. "What are you up to?"

"Nothing much. In town for a few days. Was trying to connect with this pretty lil thang, but she blew me off today for some big ass Amistad looking nigga." Lamont's bass-filled voice boisterously laughed as he planted a kiss on her forehead.

"Whatever Lamont. Since when do you just stop by my office without calling or texting? I didn't even know you were in town. And we both know you didn't come to town just for me."

"I had some last-minute business to take care of and decided to go to the barbershop. Since I was in your neigh-borhood, you were on the brain. Better yet, that ass was on the brain so I decided to see if I could um... eat a lil some-thing for lunch." He took a sip of his drink before biting the corner of his lip, examining Syncere from her bunned-crown to her sandaled soles.

Syncere would be lying if that statement and his gaze didn't make her treasure jump a little. "You nasty as fuck, Lamont." She giggled.

Brushing against her ear with his tongue, he whispered. "But you like it don't you Syncere? Tell me you like it." The heat of his breath against her ear gave her goosebumps.

"Um, yeah, you alright." She blushed.

"Alright my ass. Don't make me remind you, girl." Lamont bantered. He invited her to sit at his table and instructed the waiter to add whatever Syncere and Symphony desired to his tab.

"So, you got a new arrangement you didn't tell me about, huh?" Lamont inquired.

Syncere was bobbing her head to the music and surveying the crowd. "What new arrangement?" She questioned.

"Your new man. Dude that was in your office."

"King?" She clarified as if she was clueless. "King is not my man. It was business." Syncere kept moving to the music, taking a sip of the lemon drop martini she ordered.

"Well, it looked like a little more than business to me. Dude was burning a hole through my head in your office, just like he's doing now."

Lamont's words pulled her from her musical daze. "Staring at you now? What are you talking about Lamont?" Syncere was getting irritated because his temperament resembled a jealous boyfriend instead of a casual fuck.

"You don't see his big ass over there staring at you?" Lamont scrutinized.

Syncere scanned the room, trying to calm her heart palpitations, searching for those charcoal orbs and velvety lips. She hadn't locked eyes with him yet and she was already fluttery with anticipation. Lamont - shit, nobody had ever made Syncere feel like this - splendidly anxious, enraptured.

Syncere gazed towards the bar and there he was, holding a cognac glass, looking dangerously enticing dressed in all black. King nodded his head and lifted his drink affirming her recognition.

"You betta go say what's up to your new man," Lamont smirked.

"I never had an old man to have a new man, Lamont. Are you jealous, baby?" Syncere teased. Lamont didn't answer; he simply walked away, re-engaging with some random chick.

KING NOTICED Syncere's sparkling grey eyes and thick, pouty lips as soon as she walked through the door. He scanned her body, not certain if he was aroused or pissed off about that sheer shirt she wore, bra on display for these thirsty ass niggas. King was ready to journey towards her until he saw the dude from her office pull her into what appeared to be a comfortable caress. That hug was real close - way too familiar as if dude had a personal connection with every curve of her body. Watching Syncere with another man incensed King. He almost broke the damn cognac glass with his bare hands. He was *pissed*.

"Damn, King. You look like you ready to put a hurting on somebody." King's friend and accountant Tyus noticed his anguished disposition.

"Nah, man. I'm cool." King continued to peer in her direction, trying to determine his next move because he was definitely making a move.

Tyus followed his friend's determined line of sight. "Yo, dawg, is that her? Is that Syncere?" Tyus questioned, familiar with King's adoration for the grey-eyed beauty.

"Yeah. *That* is Syncere James." A slight blush flashed across King's Hershey chocolate face but quickly diminished once he saw Lamont nestled against her ear.

Although King and Syncere were just friendly, it didn't change the fact that he wanted that Ricky from *Boyz in the Hood* looking dude to back the fuck away from her.

Symphony was beyond tipsy - after all of that wine *and* a Major Pain, she was drunk, loud, and wrong. Her twisted halter top and crooked ass naturally curly afro disrupted Syncere's staredown with King.

"Come dance with me, Prima," Symphony shouted in Syncere's face, invading her personal space, and blocking her view of King's sexiness.

"Symphony, get your drunk ass off of me and out of my face," Syncere shouted as her cousin yanked, pulling her out of the seat to stand.

"Prima, I'm drunk and I need to dance this shit off before I let somebody's son take me home." Symphony pondered. "Well, maybe I should keep drinking." She howled. "Come on Prima, please."

"You know you've been saying that a lot tonight." Syncere rolled her eyes and mocked her cousin's voice, "*come on prima please.*"

Syncere became more motivated to dance when

Beyonce's *"Single Ladies"* blared through the speaker. The cousins pranced onto the dance floor holding hands, performing flawless Beyonce-inspired choreography. They danced through Beyonce, David Banner, Snoop Dogg, and Jay-Z until the DJ slowed down the pace. Symphony leaned against Syncere's shoulder as if she was ready to slow dance.

"Prima! Move girl. I am not getting ready to slow dance with your ass." Syncere chuckled as she started to voyage through the grinding couples.

"What's up Syncere? Symphony?" The voice of Jameson Davenport blared from behind Syncere. He was the youngest brother of Justin and Jeremiah Davenport.

"Hey, Jameson." Syncere greeted.

"Hi, Jameson. Boy, you are so damn fine." Symphony slurred as she beamed at this little young tender who was at least eight years her junior.

"I'm far from a boy, sweetheart, but thank you beautiful. Come here for a minute Symph...dance with me." Jameson tugged at her streamlined waist, not waiting for a reaction.

"Jameson, she's quite tipsy so please watch her." Syncere pleaded and he nodded his understanding.

Syncere continued to navigate her way through the crowded dance floor, wiping sweat from her brow while silently praising herself for wearing flat sandals.

"Hey, Pretty Lady." King stroked her elbow to pause her endeavor towards her seat.

"Hi, King." Her smile glittered in his presence.

"Can I have this dance?" He grazed a finger from Syncere's elbow down her forearm to hold her hand as if she'd already agreed to his offer.

"My pleasure." Syncere blushed, accepting his massive hand as he led her to the dance floor. Joe's *"I Wanna Know"* set the scene for their first dance. King gently wrapped his arms around her taut waist, positioning his sizey hands on the small of her back. He crouched a bit to make it easier for her to hug his broad neck. King smelled like sugar and spice and everything nice and nasty. His musk tantalized Syncere's senses, making her remarkably aware of the power of his embrace, the tenderness of his caress, and the curves of his muscular frame.

King inhaled her, basking in the glorious scent of honey and brown sugar. Her supple skin was smooth to his touch. King wanted to nestle into the folds of her chestnut brown neck, but he acquiesced, committing to taking it slow with her. King and Syncere were so captivated by the warmth of their collective auras that they danced through three songs, remaining bolted, intertwined. The bass of the *"Cupid Shuffle"* was the only thing to break their unspoken fantasies.

"Thank you for the dance, King," Syncere whispered, attempting to catch her breath and hurriedly exit his embrace.

"My pleasure, Princess." He sexily grinned. "Hey Syncere, can you go for a walk with me? I wanna show you something." King requested. Observing her reluctance, he cupped her chin, connecting their eyes and inquired. "Do you trust me?"

With any other man, Syncere would've deliberated on the politest way to say no, but with King, there was no hesitation. "Yes." She uttered.

King didn't mask his enthusiasm, gleaming wide,

displaying those perfectly pearly white teeth as he stroked a finger down the bridge of her nose. He guided her through the crowd and headed straight for the exit, but she first needed to inform Symphony of her departure.

"Prima, I'll be right back," Syncere whispered against Symphony's ear. "Are you good?"

"I'm good. Jameson is taking very good care of me." Symphony squealed while rubbing a hand down Jameson's chest. "You going somewhere with Lion King? Arrrgh."

Did this bitch just roar? Syncere brooded.

"Yes. We are just taking a walk. I'll be back. Don't leave me." Syncere requested.

"I got you cousin." Symphony pulled Syncere into a bear hug and sang in her ear. "*Mu-fuck-a!*"

Syncere dropped her head, trying to contain her howling laughter at her crazy cousin. King extended his hand to her, desperate to get out of Melvin's. He guided Syncere, continuing their trek across the club, hopefully uninterrupted.

"Baby girl, you good? You leaving already?" Lamont grabbed Syncere's available hand.

"Nah, I'll be back to get Symphony." *Why is Lamont trying to start some shit?* She thought.

Tightening his grip on Syncere's hand, nudging her closer to him, King leered at Lamont looking like a lion focused on its prey and ready to rip its damn head off.

"She's in good hands, dawg. Trust me." King interjected, escorting Syncere towards the door without any further consideration for Lamont.

HAVEN POINT WAS busy at this time on a Friday night. Several blocks on Main Street were blocked off, allowing pedestrian traffic to maneuver freely between the shops, restaurants, and bars. King and Syncere sauntered down the street, never relinquishing their hands.

"What did you want to show me?" She questioned.

"You'll see. It's just up the block." He continued walking, avoiding her curious gaze.

They walked the rest of the way in silence, stealing glimpses while blushing and smiling coyly. The stillness should have been awkward, but it was comfortable, refreshing - damn near euphoric.

"Here it is." King directed his head toward a vacant lot of land.

"Here what is?" Syncere's brow furrowed in confusion. "It's an empty lot."

"It's *my* empty lot. I bought it." He matter-of-factly stated.

"Why?" She was still confused. "I don't mean to be rude, but why would you buy this? This lot has divided the two neighborhoods for years. Are you trying to make Haven Point and Grover Heights become friendly?" She teased.

"Yeah, I guess that's one way to think about it." He paused, face laced with seriousness. "Grover is experiencing the same revitalization Haven did five years ago, and this piece of land could be gold in a few years. You don't agree? You're the expert, Princess."

"Well, now that you position it that way, it makes sense. But what are you going to do with it? Just let it sit until someone wants to buy it from you for five times what you paid?"

King chuckled. "Shit, that's not a bad idea. But nah, I want to open a recreation center - a place for the older kids in the neighborhood to go." He finally released Syncere's hand and moved further into the dirt-filled land. "We have parks and daycares for the little kids, dance and karate classes for the middle age kids, but it ain't shit for these teenagers to do and that's how they get in trouble. A center like what I want to build is what kept my black ass out of trouble. You feel me?" King turned, brow lifted, seeking understanding and agreement.

She was breathless. In awe of this man's thoughtfulness and candor. "Yeah King. I feel you. That is an amazing plan."

"No bullshit, Princess. Are you being serious?" He questioned.

"No. No bullshit. Real talk, that's a dope idea." Unconsciously, Syncere grabbed the hand she was missing from him. King didn't oppose.

They stood in front of the vacant lot debating on the prospective plans for the space. King and Syncere walked and talked about everything and nothing. Syncere had this abnormal feeling of vulnerability, yet perfectly secure with King. And that scared the shit out of her. This type of exchange completely defied her unwritten rules.

"I should probably get back. Check on Prima." Syncere interrupted her thought.

"Prima? Who is Prima?" King was now the one with the furrowed brow.

"Symphony. We call each other Prima. In Spanish, it

means cousin." She laughed. "It started in ninth grade and just sort of stuck."

"Ah, I get it. You and Symphony are pretty close, huh?" He questioned as he gently nudged Syncere, helping her bypass a crack in the pavement.

"Yeah, she's like my sister - my best friend." She smiled.

King and Syncere approached Melvin's still connected when they spotted Symphony and Jameson exiting the club.

"Prima!"

"Lion King!"

"Hey, y'all!" Symphony shouted as she pulled Syncere into a drunken hug.

Note to self...kill Symphony when we get home. Syncere confirmed. She embarrassingly smiled up at King, who was trying to figure out who the hell was Lion King.

"Ya girl needed some fresh air so we stepped outside to wait for you. She's drunk as shit." Jameson stated, visibly irritated by Symphony.

"Thank you, Jameson." *I'm Sorry.* Syncere mouthed. "Come on Pri, let's go, sweetie." Syncere wrapped her arm around her cousin's shoulder, ready to guide her towards the apartment.

"Princess, let me walk y'all home. You shouldn't be walking alone. Mutherfuckers get crazy on Main at this time of night." King demanded.

Syncere considered responding with her default statement, *we'll be fine,* but she knew he was right. With Symphony's head pressed against her shoulder, humming a random song, they walked the two blocks to her apartment with King following closely behind. Less than fifteen minutes later, the trio was standing in front of the building entrance.

"Prima, give me your key. I gotta pee so bad." Symphony squealed while dancing around.

"Can you make it up there without falling on your ass, Pri? And don't pee on my floor." Syncere probed while withdrawing her keys from her Louis Vuitton wristlet.

Symphony snatched the keys and darted up the one flight of stairs to her cousin's apartment, leaving Syncere and King standing in the lobby.

"Thank you for walking us home King." She began to sashay towards the steps.

"My pleasure Princess." He peered into those exemplary orbs that he adored.

"King, can I ask you a question?" He nodded. "Why do you call me princess?"

King glared deeply, admiring those portly, satiny smooth lips, desiring to snatch the Fenty Stunna lipstick right off her face. He exhaled. "I call you *princess* because you are genteel, yet feisty, sometimes timid, yet brave. You are deeply empathetic and passionate." He paused. Hands coyly stuffed in his pockets, taking a step closer to minimizing the gap between them, "Princess, you are royalty to me."

Syncere was dazed, speechless, stimulated by King's words. But what could she say other than thank you? So, she did. King recognized her anxiety intensifying. Maybe he'd overstepped - said too much, but he was done being inarticulate about his feelings. If he was going to shoot his shot, then he was going to make this shit sound off like a cannon.

"Earlier today before we were *rudely* interrupted, I wanted to ask if you're busy tomorrow." He internally flinched, prepared for her rejection.

"I have a few clients in the afternoon. But that's all. Why? What's up?"

"If you're not busy tomorrow night, I was thinking we could hang out - chill?" King confidently gazed, although his stomach was hurling.

"Um, like a date?" The thought of a real date caused Syncere's anxiety to skyrocket.

"No, not really a date. Just two friends who enjoy each other's company. Ya know, chilling over a casual dinner." He brightened.

Syncere laughed at his attempt to sell this no date philosophy, but she was curious. "Um, sure King. If it's just friends chilling right? Nothing fancy."

"Right. Nothing fancy. I can pick you up around six tomorrow." King tried to quell his elation.

"Nah playa. It's a friendly outing, remember. I can *meet* you somewhere at six. Text me the details, ok." She demanded.

"Syncere? Really?" Head cocked to the side, he glared at her, astonished that she was really serious. Syncere simply shook her head, not willing to succumb to his preference.

"I guess I'm not even going to fight you on this one, Princess." King chuckled although he was a little frustrated by her resistance.

King reached for her hand, tenderly prodding her closer, causing Syncere's heart to pound in her throat. As much as she wanted to kiss him, she had a no kissing rule - too personal. And Syncere didn't do personal. She knew that her customary noncommittal agreement wouldn't work for King - honestly, she didn't want it to work for King. He was a relationship material kind of man if Syncere did relationships. But King - shit, he had Syncere befuddled, distracted, intoxicated by his attentiveness. Experiencing feelings that were unfamiliar, concealed, and imprisoned for the past ten years.

Gently pulling her hand to his mouth for a sweet kiss, he whispered, "Goodnight Princess Syncere James."

Hand still grazing his succulent lips, she breathed, "Goodnight King Cartwright."

4

"Were you in his apartment alone after midnight, Miss James?"

"Yes, but we'd gone to a movie."

"But you were still in Mr. Dubois' apartment alone with his roommate, Mr. Quincy Parker, correct? And what were you wearing, Miss James?"

"Dean Jacobs, Quincy was in his room. I screamed for him to help me. And why does it matter what I was wearing? I'm trying to tell you Davis Dubois **raped** me."

"Think long and hard about this Miss James. Mr. Dubois has a bright future and frivolous accusations could ruin his - and yours. Maybe you're just regretting an impulsive decision. Could that be a plausible case Miss James?"

"What? Um, yeah, sure Dean Jacobs. I guess that could be it."

"Davis, please let me up. Somebody help me. Please. Davis no! Please stop!"

Syncere shuddered, crying out in her sleep for Davis to stop choking her. Legs and arms flailing, fighting for her life.

"Prima! Prima! Wake up." Symphony shouted, shaking her cousin. "Syncere, wake up. It's me. It's ok. He's not here. It's ok, Syncere."

Syncere gasped, observing the room until she locked familiar eyes with Symphony. Uncontrollably sobbing, Syncere buried her face in the pillow while Symphony climbed into the bed beside her, attempting to soothe and console her cousin. Watching Syncere experience this devastation every year was heartbreaking for Symphony. A single tear escaped her matching grey orbs, thinking back to that fateful night - recalling Syncere's disheveled clothing, smeared makeup, and blackened bruises.

The room remained still - silent. Syncere's once blaring screams were now reduced to a faint bewailing while Symphony continued to caress her brow.

"I've decided to go back to see Dr. Jacky," Syncere whispered. "I can't keep riding this emotional roller coaster. I'm exhausted, Prima. I'm so, so tired." She wept.

"Ok, Prima. Whatever you want to do." Symphony paused, wiping the stream of tears from her cousin's swollen cheeks. "You know I got you. It's going to be ok, Syncere. I promise."

A steam shower and peppermint tea, Syncere's remedy for quelling her nerves after a sleepless night. Solaced by her favorite plush white robe, Syncere was perched in the large living room bay window observing the passersby taking advantage of the beautiful summer Saturday. Symphony begged Syncere to cancel her day so they could hang out, but she had no desire to leave her apartment. Isolation would be her comfort today.

After Symphony reluctantly left to go run errands, one of Syncere's clients rescheduled their showing for today, so she decided to initiate the cancellation of the other appointment, claiming she was sick. She was definitely sick - sickened that after ten years, Davis Dubois still had control. Debilitated by the ever-present stench of his cologne. Nauseated by the heat from his breath when he forcibly kissed her. Syncere exhaled through a visible quiver when her cell phone vibrated against the table. *Prima.* She mouthed expecting her cousin to constantly check-in. She picked up the phone without viewing the number.

"I'm fine Prima. I promise. Stop worrying." Syncere blurted.

"Hey, Princess. You ok?" King's mellow yet thunderous timbre caused her quiver to return for a different reason.

"Oh, hey King. Um, yes, I'm fine." Syncere took a deep breath, attempting to sound normal.

"You sound different. You sure you're good." He queried.

"Yep. I'm fine. What's up?"

"I was calling to give you the details for tonight. Since you won't let me pick you up, you can meet me downtown-"

Shit! Syncere completely forgot about her friendly outing with King. "King, King, wait." She interrupted. "I, um - can I get a rain check?" Syncere mumbled through her statement.

"No." King matter-of-factly responded.

"Wait what? Did you say no?" Her brow creased, attitude budding.

"Yes Syncere, I said no. No, you cannot have a raincheck."

He paused, anticipating a response, but she had none. "I don't know what's bothering you and I don't need to know, but whatever it is, I promise you I can take your mind off of it."

"King." She whined.

"Princess." He rebutted, mocking her squeaky voice.

"Syncere, I'm making an executive decision. I'm coming to get you. Be ready at six." *Click*. King hung up the phone.

Syncere stared at the receiver, bewildered. *Did this man just hang up on me?* She tried to act irritated until she caught a glimpse of her face in the mirror above the dining room table. Syncere was smiling. Not a slight, uninterested smile. She was gleaming, traumatic thoughts momentarily washed away.

King cackled at the thought of Syncere's face when he hung up the phone. He knew that she was either pissed, laughing, or both. He perceived that something was bothering her, otherwise, why would her cousin be worried? King had closely observed Syncere for the past eight months. He could decipher when she was joyful, somber, infuriated - just about any emotion simply by the inflection of her voice. King desired to make sure her soft, sweet, serene voice ring in his ear permanently.

"YOU HUNG UP ON ME!" Syncere stood in her doorway, tapping her t-strap Gucci sandal against the hardwood floor, arms crossed exposing her mahogany cleavage. "Maybe I should close the door in your face, then you'll know how it feels."

"But you won't Princess." King smiled. Eying her from head to toe, struggling not to inhale too deeply, otherwise, he would devour her. "You're gorgeous." That wasn't what he intended to say but it was appropriate. She was breathtaking in a red off-the-shoulder romper exposing the single-winged butterfly tattoo on her right shoulder. Gucci crossbody to match the shoe she was still tapping, braids in a high bun, and gold hoops, identical to the silver ones she wore yesterday. King really did notice *everything* about her.

"Can I come in, Princess?" He questioned, still drinking her in.

"No." Syncere paused while King laughed, thinking she was playing, maybe revenge for his earlier behavior. "Give me a second. I need to grab my keys." She closed the door, and King quickly realized that she was serious. *Did she just lock the door while I'm standing here?* King peered around the hallway looking for the hidden cameras because he just knew he was being punked. *What the fuck?*

"I'm ready." Syncere stepped into the hallway and locked the multi-deadbolted door. King desperately wanted to inquire. *Why did she lock the door as if I wasn't standing here? Why the hell did she need so many damn locks anyway?* He understood that she lived alone, but he found her behavior strange - cautious, guarded.

Syncere turned around on her tippy-toes to find King right in her face, almost close enough to kiss. King analyzed her. His narrowed anthracite eyes feigning concern and tenderness. She struggled not to gasp as she inhaled his musky yet, honey-scented cologne.

"Are you sure you're ok, Princess?" King's gaze did not cease.

"Yes. I'm fine." She nodded.

"You mad at me?" He whispered.

"Maybe." She smirked.

"Can I make it up to you?" King uttered as he caressed her cheek, placing one hand at the small of her back.

"We'll see." Syncere broke from his embrace, sashaying down the hallway towards the stairwell, certain that King was watching.

King walked towards the lobby to head for his truck that was parked in front of her apartment building. Syncere headed in the opposite direction to the back door towards the residents' parking lot.

"Syncere, where are you going?" He curiously questioned.

"My car. I'll just follow you."

"Um, no Princess, you won't. I drove all the way over here to pick you up. You are riding with me."

"King, I would really rather take my car," Syncere whined as she continued to move towards the exit.

"Syncere." King trotted to catch up with her. "Princess, wait. What is really going on? Are you scared of me or something?"

"No. Of course not, King. Um, I just would prefer-"

"Do you trust me?" He interrupted.

Syncere did trust King, but her habits were hard to break. Besides, she didn't really date so the appropriate etiquette was unfamiliar. Syncere had never even been in Lamont's car - and she was confident that he would do her no harm. For the past five years that she'd lived alone, Lamont and one other noncommitted arrangement were the only men ever allowed in her apartment. Shit, they were the only men she'd physically been with since the rape. And it took them at least six-plus months to get an invite - in her time - within her control.

"Princess, do you trust me?" King repeated, nudging her chin, encouraging her to look at him. "Syncere, I am not going to hurt you." He affirmed, becoming acutely aware of the trepidation that resided within her. Syncere remained silent, embarrassed, trying her best not to cry. "Do-you-trust-me?" King slowly probed, lifting his brow, seeking her understanding.

"Yes, King. I trust you." Syncere nodded through a deep sigh.

King caressed her hand, pulling her towards the front exit of the building. "Let's go Pretty Lady."

The ride in the pristinely unblemished pearl white Escalade was hushed. The melodic sounds of Daniel Caesar thundered through the bass-filled speakers. King and Syncere nodded to the music, stealing glimpses and sharing sweet smiles. The guitar strings of the song *"Best Part"* gained a heightened response from Syncere. She started humming and singing, bringing delight to King's ears and a rise in his manhood. He turned down the volume, trying to eavesdrop on her heavenly voice.

"Why'd you turn it down? That's my jam." Syncere questioned.

"I can tell. I wanna hear *you* sing Princess." King blushed.

"Nah, I'm good." She chuckled. "I sing in the shower and along with the music. Never in front of people."

"It sounds like you might have some lungs over there though." His blush remained.

Syncere cleared her throat. "Mememememe." She sang as they both enthusiastically laughed.

"That's the gorgeous smile I love to see." King clutched her hand, gently kissing.

"Stop, King." Her cheeks reddened.

"Stop what, Princess?"

"Complimenting me."

King's brow furrowed. "Are you really telling me to stop complimenting you, Syncere? I don't believe that is within your control." He glared at her with slight indignation.

"I wasn't trying to be in control, King. It's just embarrassing, that's all." She shrugged, peering out of the window, noticing that they were exiting the highway towards downtown.

King didn't respond or probe as he turned into a parking garage and retrieved a ticket. He circled around a few times in silence before finding a parking space. King didn't immediately move.

"You ready King? Where are we going?" She questioned, hoping to break the awkward silence.

"Syncere, look at me." King shifted his body in the seat, waiting until their eyes connected. "It's not my intention to embarrass you or make you uncomfortable. I think you're beautiful and I love to see you smile - so if it's on my heart, I'm going to tell you so. Are you ok with that?"

King was proving to continually render Syncere breathless, captivated - shit, turned the fuck on. "Yes. Yeah, I'm ok with that?" She stuttered.

"Ok then. Our first stop is The Park." He finally responded to her initial question as he exited the truck. Rounding the back of the SUV to approach the passenger side, he noticed Syncere was trying to open her door so he quickly pushed the door lock button on the key fob.

"King, I'm trying to get out." She shouted through the closed window, watching as he approached the passenger door. King unlocked the door and then opened it for her. Syncere stepped out, boxed in by his massive limbs.

"Princess, I have a few rules of my own. When you are with me, I open doors, pull out chairs, offer compliments, pay for everything. I am a gentleman - and it's non-negotiable. Are we clear?"

"Clear." Syncere jokingly saluted.

"So, let's roll." He declared.

Syncere clutched the hand King extended to her, following him towards the garage's pedestrian exit. The assertiveness of King's words had her legs clenched tightly, attempting to desist her pulsating treasure. His actions were not an act of control or authority, but a gesture of protection - something he sensed she unknowingly desired.

SIMILAR TO MAIN Street in Haven Point, the downtown streets were crowded and spirited. Sounds of live music and the delightful smells from the food trucks filled the nighttime air.

"King? You said our first stop?" She probed. "How many stops are we making?"

"As many as we want. Let's have some fun tonight, okay?" King winked.

King and Syncere entered an area called The Park where rows of food trucks lined the repurposed parking lot. American, Chinese, Mexican, Italian - just about every specialty you craved was available. A live cover band, round tables, and chairs were positioned in the center with fully stocked bars at each end.

"Have you ever been here before?" King inquired, opening the gate for her to enter.

"No. I rarely get downtown. This is amazing though." She squealed.

"So, what's your pleasure? Are you in the mood for a burger, pizza, pasta - take your pick?" He twisted around pointing out the visible options.

"Hmmm, so much to choose from. I think I want a combination of things." Syncere chuckled.

"Ha! Okay. Do you, Princess."

"What are you going to get, King?"

"I think I want to keep it simple. I'll probably get a burger. Have you decided?" He paused, catching a glimpse of Syncere's wide eyes. "What? What's wrong?"

"Be still my heart, King." She clasped her hands across her chest. "There's a funnel cake truck." She gleamed. "That might be my dinner - like for real."

King heartily laughed at her silliness. He enjoyed seeing her like this - relaxed and carefree. "Like I said, do you beautiful."

Syncere decided to get a chicken sandwich from the same truck as King, but sweet potato waffle fries from another truck. They found seats towards the back, away from the band so they could chat.

"What are you drinking?" King asked.

"Um, I'll stick with water." Syncere usually enjoyed an alcoholic beverage but would never partake socially unless she was with her cousin.

"Syncere, are you sure you don't want a lemon drop?" He blushed.

"King, how do you know-?" She snickered. "Nevermind." Syncere tossed her hand at him, still laughing.

"I'm glad you're catching on, Princess. Like I said, I remember everything about you." He winked. "Now, do you want a drink?"

"Yes, King. A lemon drop sounds wonderful. Thank you." She blushed.

King was not kidding about making as many stops as they wanted. After eating and enjoying the music at The Park, they walked a block to the bowling alley where Syncere boasted about beating King twice.

"King, I promise I won't tell your boys that I beat you at not one, but two games. " Throwing up two fingers, she haughtily cackled.

"I was just having an off night because you're so beautiful, Princess." He chortled.

"Nah, playa. I beat that ass." Syncere's resounding angelic laughter caused King to stare as they aimlessly ambled through the streets holding hands.

"Princess, are you ready for a surprise?" King blurted, disrupting her continuous laughter.

"Surprise? Rule number 314 - I don't like surprises." Syncere joked as she shoved King but his robust frame was unmovable.

"Well, rules are made to be broken." He collapsed his arms around her shoulders, pulling her into a forehead kiss. "Let's go, pretty lady."

They walked back towards The Park, hands still connected, as King grinned sneakily once they approached a white horse-drawn carriage illuminated with soft yellow lights.

"Your chariot awaits, Princess." King extended his arm and directed her towards the carriage.

"King, are you serious?" Syncere gasped, sparkling with exhilaration.

King and Syncere toured downtown cuddled in the plush red velvet carriage seats. Her face was radiant, gorgeous gray orbs glistening with that immense angelic smile. King wanted to kiss her - so he fulfilled his wish.

King captured her lips with a delicate and tender kiss, momentarily withdrawing to forecast potential opposition from Syncere. Seeing none, he parted her lips with his searing plump tongue, invading her mouth with his full lips. He stroked the curves of her face with one hand while caressing the nape of her neck. They were lost in that kiss - moaning, disoriented, and salacious.

"King." Syncere whimpered. "King, I -" She had no words.

"You what Princess? Do you want me to stop?" He paused, gazing while still fondling her satiny skin.

"No. No, don't stop." Syncere shocked her damn self while endearing the muscular contour of his face. It had been countless years since the last time she was kissed. And a lifetime since a kiss had her toes curling, goosebumps rising, and a sodden wet treasure. Kissing was not a part of her noncommittal agreements, but Syncere was experiencing everything but lack of commitment with King. She felt trust-worthiness, devotion, fidelity - secure.

Slowly yet urgently stroking each other's face, their tongues intertwined in the most splendid dance. King briefly relinquished her luscious lips, allowing his tongue to explore her sweet floral-scented neck. He was discombobulated, intoxicated by her aroma and the flavor of her supple mouth.

"King." She mumbled through her delicious wail. "King, we-we should stop." Syncere was captivated, impassioned - shit, insanely aroused but cautious. The carriage ride concluded with King and Syncere still entwined, not ready to release.

"Come on Princess. I want to show you your next surprise." He apprehended her lips one more time.

"More surprises?" She questioned, still reeling from that kiss.

"Yes, more Princess." He declared, kissing the back of her hand.

King helped Syncere out of the carriage, placing a hand on her waist, escorting her towards the next surprise. As they walked on the cobblestone pavement, Syncere noticed the flashing of kaleidoscopic-colored lights illuminating the sky.

After a few more steps, the colossal ferris wheel was in view. King's eyes were brightened by the expression on Syncere's face - a combination of excitement and distress.

"Um, King. I'm not so sure about this." She mumbled.

"Princess, it's fine. You said you trust me, right." He cupped her face, connecting orbs.

"Yeah well, maybe I was mistaken." She nervously chuckled while she hesitantly followed him.

"Good evening. We have a private gondola reserved for Cartwright." King spoke to the agent while Syncere clutched his hand tighter, tossing her head back between her shoulders to take in the height of the massive wheel. *Oh my God.* She mouthed in awe.

"Princess, I got you. I promise." King assured. Syncere nodded with no words.

They stepped into the private gondola and Syncere immediately noticed the bottle of champagne, two champagne flutes, plush brown leather seats, and a glass-bottom floor.

"King! The floor is see-through." She leered, still focused on the glass floor. "What in the world did I get myself into?"

King couldn't control his hearty guffaw. Wishing he could capture the expression on her face.

"King, it's not funny." She pouted.

"Syncere, are you scared for real? We don't have to go, Princess, if you're afraid." King set aside the jokes to ensure she was comfortable.

"I'm fine." She paused. "But if I scratch a hole in your damn arms, it's your fault." She glared at King, her expression laced with seriousness.

"Whatever you need, pretty lady. But it's going to be fun. I promise." King winked.

"You make a lot of promises Mr. Cartwright." Syncere skeptically peered at him.

"Trust me. I keep my promises, Miss James." King ensured that he was staring directly into those suspicion-filled eyes so there was no confusion.

The 30-minute ride was fascinating, offering a beautiful view of the city lights. Syncere sipped her champagne, unbothered by the glass floor; in fact, she sauntered around the gondola taking in the scenery from different angles, relishing the experience. The couple exited the gondola with matching redden cheeks.

"See, that wasn't so bad Princess," King confirmed.

"It was breathtaking, King." Syncere squealed, wrapping her arms around his Herculean frame. The voluntary warm-hearted action caught both King and Syncere by surprise. They gazed at each other, flirtatiously grinning, time seemingly endless.

"We should probably head back unless you're ready for more surprises." King chortled.

"Nah, I think I've had all I can handle for one night." She coyly smiled.

King and Syncere returned to the carriage, riding in silence while she rested her head on his shoulder until they reached the garage.

The car ride home was equally hushed, but not awkwardly so. King rubbed a thumb across the palm of her hand, as she leaned in his direction, one leg folded under the other in the passenger seat. This is exactly what King craved, moments like this with his princess.

They arrived at Syncere's apartment around 1 am. She was visibly exhausted - yawning and nodding.

"Princess, you're home." King gently nudged her awake.

He exited the truck, ambling to the passenger side to open her door. King extended his hand, helping her out of the truck, her to-go funnel cake in tow. He walked Syncere up the one flight of stairs to her apartment. Keys in hand, she didn't immediately unlock the door.

"I had a good time tonight. Thanks, King." She sleepily whispered.

"My pleasure Princess." He smiled, planting a sweet kiss on her cheek. "I'll wait here. I want to make sure you're in safely." He nodded his head towards the door, signaling her to unlock it. Taking a large step back, he uttered, "Go ahead, I won't crowd you." Recalling her earlier behavior, he sensed that she needed the space.

Syncere unlocked the three locks then crossed the threshold into her apartment. "Goodnight King." She uttered as she slowly closed the door.

"Goodnight Princess." He whispered as the door shut and the click of the first lock resounded.

King was floating like in a Spike Lee movie. As much as he tried, he couldn't relinquish the monumental grin on his face. Meanwhile, Syncere was on a Spike Lee Joint too, sailing across her living room into the bedroom - they were euphoric, giddy. Syncere texted King requesting that he inform her when he made it home. He obliged.

King: Hey Princess. I'm home.

Princess: Glad you made it safely.

King: Thank you. I pray you have delightful dreams, Princess.

Princess: Ditto. ;)

King snickered, expecting that type of response from her. Meanwhile, Syncere beamed, drifting off to sleep, slumbering all night for the first time in weeks.

5

Syncere arose well-rested on Monday morning after spending Saturday night with King and exchanging texts and phone calls on Sunday. She was working from home today since she would be reunited with Dr. Jacky this afternoon and was uncertain of the emotional roller coaster she would potentially face. Dr. Jaclyn Bernard Valdez was a licensed psychologist who specialized in rape and sexual assault trauma.

Syncere was anxious about visiting Dr. Jacky again because she knew that the good doctor would not be pleased with the almost two-year hiatus from therapy. But, Syncere desperately needed to get reacquainted with the calming methods that previously helped her through the PTSD. *King seems to be a pretty good way to keep me calm.* She mused, blushing at the thought of King's attention, thoughtfulness-and those damn silky lips.

"Whew Lord! That man is going to be the death of me."

She pondered aloud, padding across her living room into the kitchen, searching the refrigerator for something to eat that didn't require a pot or pan. The blare of her cell phone broke her daze. Syncere tapped the button on her wireless earbuds to answer the call.

"Good morning Prima." She squealed.

"Good morning Princess." King's guttural morning voice sent a shiver down her spine. "Tell me what's required for me to put that kind of smile on your face in anticipation of my call." He snickered.

Little did he know, he was the primary reason for her glistening beam and pattering heart.

"Good morning King. I'm just so used to Symphony calling me around this time every day." She chuckled. "How's your morning?"

"It was great until I stopped by the office and you weren't there. Is everything ok?" He questioned.

"Yeah, everything is fine. I'm working from home today. I have a doctor's appointment later." Syncere decided not to share specifics.

Finding nothing of interest to eat, she footed across the living room to her favorite place, the seated bay window. The booming sound of machinery pounding the pavement quickened her time at the window. She was having difficulty hearing King but was unsure if it was her surroundings or his.

"King, where are you? Your background is really loud." She curiously probed.

"Sorry, Princess. I'm walking out of the Brown Bean and they're doing some work on the street. Can you open your door in about five minutes? I have your coffee and croissant."

"King." She shouted. "What? I'm not dressed." Syncere tightly clasped the belt of her robe as if he could see her. "And I'm a mess."

"I highly doubt that Princess." He sexily grinned as he pondered her gorgeous features. "Syncere, I'm not trying to come in. I just figured you wanted breakfast."

Syncere reflected on her behavior when King picked her up on Saturday. She was certain that he thought she'd lost her mind - multiple locks on the door, making him stand outside instead of inviting him in. Syncere was often crippled by her anxiety-riddled behaviors, preventing her from having real attachments aside from her grandmother and cousin. She could already hear Dr. Jacky's melodic yet firm tone recommending she trust her intuition. Syncere's insight was speaking loud and clear - *give King a chance,* but would she listen.

The light thump against her front door disrupted her attempt to fix the messy braided bun on top of her head. Syncere threw on some leggings and a t-shirt, opting to discard the robe since she decided to invite King in - if he desired.

"Hi, King." Syncere unsuccessfully tried to temper the massive curve of her lips, examining the way his crisp white dress shirt embraced his physique.

"Hi, Princess. Good morning." King beamed - making no attempt to quell the goosebumps her gorgeous fresh face produced. "Here you go pretty lady- one coffee, one crois-sant." He extended his arms across the threshold, careful not to step inside, handing over the Brown Bean-logoed bag and coffee cup.

"Thank you, King."

"My pleasure. Well, I'll talk to you later, okay. Have a good day." As much as he longed to spend the morning with her, he needed Syncere to desire his presence.

"Do you - would you like to come in?" Syncere stuttered, interrupting King, offering an invitation while she had the nerve.

"Come in? To your spot?" King inquired, stunned by her offer. "Um, yeah. I mean, if you're sure, Princess."

"Yes, I'm sure. Come in." Syncere stepped aside, allowing him to enter her foyer.

KING OBSERVED the massive loft-like apartment. There were four apartments in the Davenport building and Syncere's was the largest, spanning the entire half of the second floor. He momentarily thought he was dreaming - often curious about her private oasis. It was exactly as he imagined. The modern structure was complemented by a farmhouse glam design. Variant brown and gray furniture throughout, with hints of yellow, purple, and blue accents. The huge bay window with a plush cushioned seat was the center of attention in the space, providing a spectacular view of Haven Point.

"Would you like a plate for your breakfast?" Syncere's voice echoed from the kitchen, pulling King from his trance.

"Um, yeah, that's cool." He shortened their separation,

taking a seat at the kitchen island. "So, this is Syncere's sanctuary, huh?" He winked.

"Something like that, I guess." She shrugged, placing the glass plate on the island. "Your home should be your sanctuary, right?"

"Absolutely. You have a nice place though, Princess. How long have you lived here?"

"Five years. When I started working for Davenport, they'd just finished renovating this apartment and I fell in love. It was time for me and Symphony to get our own spaces so she stayed in our childhood home and I got this place. It's been perfect for me." Syncere leaned against the counter opposite King, peering around the apartment, recollecting the time when she finally was strong enough - secure enough to live alone.

"Well, I appreciate you for inviting me in. Thank you, Princess." King's reverberating voice infringed her reminiscing.

"Thanks for bringing me coffee." She blushed, blowing to cool her perfectly brewed java before taking a sip.

"Don't forget the croissant. I had to fight off an old lady to get that damn thing." He teased.

"You didn't have to go through the trouble just for me." Syncere giggled. "The battle for those croissants is no joke at this time of the morning."

"*Only* for you Princess." He stressed. "I wouldn't go through the trouble for anybody else - but you..." King gazed directly into her rested orbs, leaving no uncertainty of his affection.

Syncere was embarrassed again, feeling unworthy of

King's advances. She was just unassured if she could consistently be what he wanted, needed - deserved.

King could always sense when Syncere was in her head - anxious and uncertain, so he decided he wouldn't push the conversation.

"I can't stay long Princess. I need to get to the office." King stood to his full height, minimizing her frame, and took the last bite of his sandwich, washing it down with iced coffee.

"Ok. Thank you again, King. I appreciate you." She began further closing the gap between them, walking towards the island to discard the trash. But she wasn't close enough for King's liking.

"Can I have a hug before I go?" He flirtatiously smiled, stroking a finger down the bridge of her nose. She obliged, wrapping her arms around his brawny waist. Syncere inhaled his sandalwood musk for a second too long. Her traitorous treasure was so damn saturated, she was certain he could smell her sugary nectar simmering from her thong.

He did - and he was inebriated, drunk from the candied scent. King wanted to taste Syncere so fucking bad. He abruptly disconnected from her embrace, feeling the pressure from his dick about to explode. Syncere didn't fully disengage, leaning her head back, digesting the dark chocolatey goodness of his skin, catching another glimpse of him before he departed. King bit the side of his lip, desperately needing to exit immediately. His brain told him to leave - exit stage left now, but his feet were woefully uncooperative, fastened to her slate hardwood floors. Syncere's irises glistened like shooting stars, her lips lustrous like precious gems that he had to capture.

King kissed her softly, sweetly while her hands unhurriedly navigated up the curves of his chest, caressing the nape of his neck. He inhaled her, licking her lips with his hazelnut-flavored tongue. Biting, nibbling, their tongues partaking in a delicious game of tug of war. King's massive hands roamed the length of her body, tenderly kneading her beautifully plump ass. He effortlessly lifted her onto the marble countertop, and Syncere graciously wrapped her ample thighs around his waist.

King's mouth never detached, his hands continued their exploration, creeping up her t-shirt, unhooking the front closure bra, releasing her gloriously round breasts. He marveled at the sight of her luminous mocha mounds. Manipulating, stroking, squeezing, giving equal attention to each one. But he longed the flavor of her mahogany skin on his tongue. Trailing kisses down her neck, he engulfed her breast, one by one, delicately, yet firmly nibbling her darkened, swollen nipples.

"Ahh shit, King." She moaned, tenderly massaging her fingers through his thick, groomed beard. King's dick was aching for Syncere, but at that moment he would've been satisfied with just a taste of her succulent juices. His exploration continued, fingering the waist of her leggings, nudging them down to her thighs, exposing a sexy black thong that temporarily concealed her dripping treasure. King was anxious, hurried - he contemplated ripping the thong from her flesh. He caressed, stroked, and fondled her treasure with his palm, feeling the heated juices penetrate the silky material.

ROBBI RENEE

"Princess, you're so damn wet. Is all of this for me?" He sexily grinned against her shivering lips.

Syncere was breathless, trying to locate a response when the sounds of *"I Always Love My Mama"* blared from her cell phone.

Shit! "King. King." She moaned.

"Yes, Princess. Please don't tell me to stop." He begged.

"King. You have to stop. I need to answer that." King peered around, trying to understand what the fuck she was saying because he was pleasantly disoriented.

"King, I gotta answer my phone. It's my grandmother." She whispered against his ear, his hand still grazing her treasure. Syncere involuntarily surrendered from his extraordinarily tender grasp. Hopping off of the counter, she fixed her disheveled clothes as if G-ma could see her through the phone.

"Hey, G-ma. Um, good morning." Syncere mumbled through an exhale as salacious sensations traveled down her spine.

"Good morning girly girl. Are you busy?"

Shit! I was trying to get busy. She mused, not paying much attention to her grandmother. Syncere's eyes were concentrated on King as he rubbed his thumb across his lush lips. She surveyed him, observing the monumental bulge pressed against the zipper of his olive-colored slacks.

"Syncere, are you ok? You're breathing hard." G-ma's voice disrupted her visual feast.

"Yeah, G-ma. I'm ok. Are you ok?" Syncere hadn't disconnected her eyes from King's anthracite orbs or his concealed dick.

"I'm fine baby. I was just calling to tell you good luck with Dr. Jacky today."

Syncere momentarily relinquished King's gaze, comprehending her grandmother's words.

"Symphony talks too much. G-ma, I was going to tell you. I promise I was." Syncere whined.

"Don't you worry about that. I'm thankful you're going back. You've missed out on so much Syncere... staying all bottled up." G-ma sighed. "Just make sure you call me later, ok? You know I'm praying."

"Yes ma'am. I know. I love you." Syncere briefly exchanged pleasantries then hung up, pausing for a brief moment to suppress her antsy-ness and throbbing treasure.

"King, I'm sorry-" He interrupted, placing a finger over her lips to silence her words.

"No need to apologize, Princess." He licked his lips, tasting remnants of her vanilla flavored tongue. "Walk me to the door." King grabbed her hand, hesitantly footing towards the exit. He didn't want to go, but he acquiesced, unlocking every barrier before turning around to give her one last kiss.

"Call me later if you wanna talk, ok." He whispered against her lips. "Have a good day, pretty lady."

"Ok." That's all she had - no words, unable to craft a coherent sentence, he rendered her voiceless. Syncere closed the door, leaning against it for balance - legs wobbly and treasure blazing. "Fuck!" Her shout echoed from the vaulted ceiling.

———

SYNCERE TOOK an extra-long steamy shower after her morning encounter with King. She was in disbelief that she allowed it to happen - on her damn kitchen counter no less. Syncere had a list of things she needed to discuss with Dr. Jacky and King just made it to the top. She couldn't comprehend how all of her rules, noncommittal agreements, and lack of intimacy evaporated into thin air in King's presence. With Lamont, there was no intimacy, only sex - good sex nonetheless, but scheduled and regimented. Something she habitually craved, but lately, Lamont was an afterthought.

Syncere scrambled through her apartment, running late for her appointment. She practically jumped into a pair of jeans, a fitted black t-shirt, and a comfy pair of leopard-print Rothy's. Fresh-faced, she rushed out of the apartment, locked the door when her phone blared. This time she checked the name, verifying the caller, wishing it was King, but it was her cousin.

"Bitch, why'd you tell G-ma about my appointment with Dr. Jacky?" Syncere yelled.

"Bitch what? Now you know G-ma is best friend number two. I tell her everything." Symphony whined.

"Well tell her your damn business. Why does it seem like she always knows my shit?" Syncere trotted down the steps, pulling the phone away to check the time. *Shit.* "Prima, I gotta go. I'm late and you know the good doctor don't play that."

"Oooh, you know she hates that. You didn't work today. Why are you so late?" Symphony questioned.

"Since you are no longer my favorite cousin, I'm not telling you. And it's some juicy tea too." Syncere squealed, doing a little shimmy as she hopped in her silver Lexus GX.

"Juicy? Prima, please tell me. I need some juicy drama in my boring ass life." Symphony held the phone against her shoulder as she reviewed medical charts while at work. "Syncere, I'm listening."

"Boring? What about baby boy Jameson or old man Clyde?" Syncere probed.

"Heffa, his name is Calvin, and 52 is not that old."

"It is when your ass is 32." Syncere cackled.

"Whatever! And as for Jameson - he is a fine ass, grown-ass man in the sheets, boo, soooo..." Symphony's voice trailed off.

"Unnn - you nasty with yo baby boy and old man river loving ass." Syncere blaringly howled. "But anyway, Prima, promise me this doesn't become Friday night tea with G-ma?" She pleaded.

"Cross my heart and hope to die, stick a needle in my eye. Spill it." Symphony crossed her fingers over her heart to seal the promise.

"Um, King brought me coffee this morning." Syncere blushed.

"Heffa, King brings you coffee all the time. How is this juicy tea?" Symphony interjected.

"If you would let me finish, damn. Like I said, King brought me coffee...into my apartment."

"Awww shit!" Symphony screeched.

"Prima!" Syncere shouted.

"Ok, ok, ok. I'm sorry. Continue. Lion King - coffee - apartment - go."

"Ugh! You really get on my nerves." Syncere rolled her eyes, irritation apparent through her voice. "We had breakfast in my apartment. He couldn't stay long but asked for a hug before he left. That hug turned into me on the counter, his tongue down my throat, bra unfastened, his hands all over my treasure."

"What! Did Lion King *mu-fuck-a* you?" Symphony's high pitched squeals echoed through the car speakers.

"No! We didn't have sex, Prima." Syncere laughed.

"Well, why the hell not? You let that man go to work with blue balls while your ass was sitting there with ya titties hanging?"

"First of all, bitch, my titties don't hang. And thanks to you, we were interrupted by G-ma calling to wish me luck at Dr. Jacky's today." Syncere paused, waiting for her cousin's reaction.

"Oh shit. My bad. I'm sorry, Prima."

"No need to apologize. I was saved by the bell. I can't go there with King anyway." That potential reality brought sadness to Syncere's heart.

"Um, let me ask again - why the hell not?" Symphony loudly inquired.

"I'm pulling into the parking lot so I can't get into this with you today. But the bottom line is, King is not, cannot - shit, won't be a noncommittal agreement." Syncere shrugged, trying to convince herself more than her cousin.

"Well Prima, let me leave you with this. Maybe it's time to let that noncommittal bullshit go because trust me when I tell you, if you told Lamont today that you wanted a relationship, he would drop everything. That noncommitment shit is *you*, Prima - not them. It's your fake way to protect yourself. And King? Whew, chile - every bitch in Haven is checking for his fine ass so fuck it up if you want to." Symphony paused. "Prima, I pray you have a good appointment and that you allow yourself to be vulnerable and honest. If you do that - you will be fine."

Syncere sighed, "Thanks *Iyanla.* I hate you, but I love you."

"I love you too, boo," Symphony whispered, disheartened that her cousin didn't feel deserving of a man like King and couldn't see the magnificent opportunity for love staring her in the face.

6

Entering Dr. Jacky's office, she heard the familiar soothing sound of the makeshift waterfall against the calming soft yellow painted wall. The receptionist pleasantly greeted Syncere, peering at the clock to check the time. "Dr. Jacky is wrapping up. She'll be right with you."

Syncere unleashed a sigh of relief since she wasn't late. But that didn't dismiss the nerves and anxiety she was experiencing. So much had transpired over the past few weeks from debilitating nightmares to an unforgettable friendly outing and a mind-blowing kiss - among other things. Over the last few days, Syncere hadn't experienced any nightmares - drifting to sleep with King's raspy timbre or tender text messages wishing her a peaceful night. But she knew that his big heart and powerful frame wasn't enough to fully protect her. Syncere needed to protect herself in healthy ways - not the noncommittal barriers she created over the past ten years. The chime of her phone broke her daze.

King: Hi Princess. I was just thinking about you. I hope you're having a good day and your appointment is going well. Call me later if you get a chance. I have a proposition for you.

Syncere grinned, responding, *Hi King. I'm in the doctor's office but I'll call you later. Hmmm a proposition. What are you up to now?? I'm nervous. :)*

She was extremely curious about King's proposition but Dr. Jacky's tall, slender frame brought her to attention. Syncere glanced at her phone noticing a response from King.

King: No need to be a nervous Princess. I promise it's good. ;)

"Well hello, Miss Syncere. Did you forget the drill, my dear? Go ahead and give your phone to Sandra. You'll get your lifeline back when we're done." Dr. Jacky's firm declaration disrupted her blushing.

Syncere powered off her phone and simply nodded her understanding as she removed her shoes, remembering that policy before entering Dr. Jacky's sanctum.

Dr. Jacky's office screamed unapologetic black girl magic. Degrees from Howard University, paintings of beautiful black women of all hues dressed the walls, bookshelves filled with the legendary writings of Maya Angelou, Audre Lorde, Nikki Giovanni, Toni Morrison, Ntozake Shange, and countless others. African artifacts from her travels are meticulously displayed throughout the room.

Syncere preferred the oversized blush-colored chair instead of the couch for her sessions. She took a seat, crossing her legs under her, sipping on the peppermint tea she made while in the waiting area.

Dr. Jacky looked visually different, trading her long, flowing hair for a short pixie cut, and Prada tortoise frames now concealed her hazel eyes. But her methods remained the same, opening the session in prayer.

"Dear Heavenly Father, please grant us peace of mind during this session today. Calm any troubled hearts and spirits. Give Syncere the strength and clarity of mind to find her purpose and walk the path you've laid out for her. We trust you with our lives today. Thank God and Amen."

"Amen," Syncere whispered as she wiped away a single tear that escaped the thunderous clouds forming in her eyes.

"Take a breath, Syncere." Dr. Jacky deeply inhaled modeling the behavior. "What is that all about?" She circled her figure, pointing towards Syncere.

"What is what about?" Syncere coyly responded.

"My dear, we are not even ten minutes into our session and you're ready to cry. Did you think you were in trouble?" Dr. Jacky giggled and Syncere joined.

"Kinda. Yeah, I guess so." She cackled. "I'm just nervous. So much has happened since the last time we talked."

"Ok, well start from where we left off." Dr. Jacky sat patiently listening to Syncere speak about her success at Davenport Realty, her grandmother's health, Lamont, the nightmares, and King. Miraculously, Dr. Jacky never took copious notes during her sessions. She was always locked in, focused, listening to her clients.

"I want to mix up the order a bit and focus on the nightmares. It sounds like they've changed a little over time, is that accurate?"

"Changed how? He still violates me. So how has that changed?" Syncere's creased forehead indicated confusion.

"Violate? That's what you're calling it now?" Dr. Jacky peeked over her glasses. "And who is he? You have to name it and name him, my dear."

"Davis Dubois. He - Davis still rapes me at the end of every nightmare, so how has it changed?" Syncere blew out a cheek-filled breath.

"Close your eyes and take a second to think about how you described the nightmares the last time we met compared to today." Dr. Jacky never disjoined her eyes from Syncere.

Syncere pondered the doctor's words, playing the horrid events over in her head. In the past, her nightmares focused on the rape itself - the choking, slapping, the vaginal trauma, whereas recent remembrances extended to the aftermath. The painful walk home, the cold shower to soothe the sting, reporting to campus police, the meeting with Dean Jacobs. Syncere's body visibly quaked, the burdensome inquiry on repeat in her spirit. *Are you certain it was rape Miss James?*

"I guess the nightmares are less about being raped and more about them not -" She paused, eyes narrowed, legs quivering, breathing labored.

"Who are they Syncere?" Dr. Jacky questioned. "Name it. Name them. Say it again."

"The nightmares are less about me being raped by Davis and more about the campus police and Dean Jacobs not believing me. Questioning if I wanted it - if I was really raped. They focused on what I was wearing instead of the bruises." Syncere's lips trembled, holding in the vehement wail that was brewing.

"Release, my dear. Let your heart break Syncere." Dr. Jacky whispered.

"I'm exhausted, Dr. Jacky." Syncere's eyes were lifeless, she was numb. "I'm tired of crying, blaming myself, tired of thinking about the way Davis slapped me, the way Dean Jacobs dismissed me. I just want to move forward."

"And why haven't you moved forward in the last ten years, my dear?" Dr. Jacky asked, but continued talking, not seeking an answer. "You have a successful career, a great relationship with your G-ma, your prima. But what about everybody else? Hmm?" She peeked over her glasses again. "You've spent so much time *thinking* instead of feeling, that you don't know how to just let your heartbreak, my dear. What do you call it - the noncommittal agreement you had with Marcus and now Lamont? My dear, it hurts you more than it hurts him."

"How? How does it hurt me when I'm the one in control? Lamont is on my time, my discretion. No feelings to consider, no hearts being broken. That's why I let Marcus go. He was trying to get too close." Syncere's attitude progressed by the minute.

"So, it's about control then?" Dr. Jacky's frustrating smirk was pissing off Syncere.

She hopped out of the plush chair and hurried to the window, similar to her apartment's bay window but without a seat. "Yes, it's about control," Syncere shouted, the tear-filled cloud finally breaking free. "Yes! I say what, how, when, and who. It's *my* schedule, not theirs - *my* consent."

"Because Davis had all of the control. Is that accurate?"

"He had a plan and he successfully executed. The pursuit, the flirting, the date, the phone call from Quincy, everything. He said it best - Davis gets what Davis wants...and he did. So, you see Dr. Jacky, the agreements I've had, they protect me from men like Davis." Syncere aggressively wiped her tears, returning to her chair, avoiding eye contact.

"My dear, you have been broken, heart shattered, soul wounded, and your coping mechanism is defending yourself - hence your attitude with me." That frustrating smirk resurfaced as she continued. "Creating these arbitrary agreements, giving you the illusion that you have control. When in reality my dear, you are out of control, spiraling."

"I'm out of control? Oh - okay." With her arms crossed over her chest, Syncere was outwardly furious, but internally, she knew Dr. Jacky was right.

"So, my dear, how does this gentleman, King, feel about that? The agreement. Hmm?" Syncere's dewy indignant grey orbs shot up, leering at the good doctor.

"King is not an agreement. King is -" Her voice trailed off, a slight smile forming. "He's my friend."

"Well, he sounds like an amazing friend." Dr. Jacky smiled but Syncere knew it was some other shit behind that smile. "My dear, you experienced life-altering trauma, there's no doubt about it. The pain, bruises, hurt, humiliation will always be a part of your story, but it doesn't have to be the whole story. There can be beauty in your brokenness, Syncere." Dr. Jacky searched Syncere's misty eyes for understanding. "Syncere, your rape has caused you to compartmentalize your feelings. You still love and care deeply for your grandmother, your cousin, anyone who was in your life before the rape. After the trauma, every relationship has been a transaction that you could control, just like selling a house. But my dear, as long as you continue to believe that these agreements are working, that sex without intimacy or relationship is the norm, Davis will always be in control. And every man is *not* like Davis."

Syncere audibly exhaled, deflating her air-filled cheeks. "This feels like the longest 90 minutes of my life." Syncere self-consciously grinned, still inhaling and exhaling to practice her breathing.

Dr. Jacky intently smiled in her special way. "Well, I believe you did good work here today my dear. You're a smart, intuitive woman, Syncere, but you must allow your head and your heart to align. It could lead you towards the possibility of something, or someone, that you never imagined could be an essential part of your healing." She winked.

"I hear you and I understand you, Dr. Jacky. I'll see you in two weeks?" Syncere smiled.

"I will be here if the Lord says so." Dr. Jacky's session ending statement hadn't altered either. Syncere grabbed her shoes and purse heading to the door when the good doctor continued. "Oh, and Syncere, we'll talk more about King *and* Mariah next time."

Syncere's smile momentarily faltered. "Ok, Dr. Jacky. It won't be pretty but I will be ready." She confidently confirmed.

SYNCERE WAS SO thankful the rest of her day was clear to digest and reflect on her session with Dr. Jacky. She stopped at the local deli *Sliced and Diced* to grab a chicken salad wrap, broccoli and cheddar soup, and their famous cream soda that was brewed and bottled in-house. Syncere had no intentions of leaving her apartment for the rest of the day. She called G-ma and Symphony as promised, changed into her red silky pajamas, copped-a-squat on the velvety plush grey chaise, and popped the glass bottle of cream soda.

Syncere wasn't sullen or dejected, actually, she felt alleviated, mending - happy that she was open, honest, and transparent during her session. Dr. Jacky didn't have to give Syncere a homework assignment for her to start journaling. It was a part of the good doctor's requirements for her patients.

Syncere devoured her food, realizing that she'd only had coffee and a croissant all day. The thought invited King's splendidly statuesque frame to the forefront. He asked her to call but she was hesitant after the heaviness of her day. *I'm sure he's too busy to talk to me anyway.* She tried to reason but instead made excuses.

Little did she know, King was still in the neighborhood at a construction site, hoping that she would call before he headed home. He desperately desired an invitation back to Syncere's apartment; not to finish what they started, but to simply be with her. King checked his phone to find no texts or messages from Syncere. His workers dispersed, the day turned to night, and King was drained. It was time for him to go home. King contemplated calling her, but he made his intentions clear. If Syncere wanted to talk, she knew where to find him.

King lived in the Bridgeport Hills neighborhood, about twenty minutes north of Haven Point. He pulled into his garage when his phone rang through the car speaker. He glanced at the dashboard screen, expecting to see *My Princess* on the display, but the caller ID was a disappointment.

"What's up, bro?" King answered.

"Ain't shit happening. What's going on with you, bro? You still at work?" King's friend Tyus inquired.

"Nah, I just got home, man. I'm tired as fuck though." King yawned, grabbing his phone to disconnect the call from the car's Bluetooth. "What's up dawg?" King disengaged his house alarm and was greeted by his charcoal grey French Bulldog named Zeus.

"Are we still good for this weekend?" Tyus questioned. "I'm ready to turn the fuck up for my 35th birthday."

"You act like it ain't Titan's birthday too. What are y'all like 14 minutes apart?" King teased. "But yeah, man, everything is set. The house will be ready by 3 pm, but I probably won't even be able to leave the city until two o'clock. Does that work for y'all?"

King was planning to spend the weekend in Brighton Falls to celebrate his friends, twin brothers Tyus and Titan's birthday. Brighton Falls was about a two-hour drive from Haven Point, a popular summer getaway. King's family owned a house on the lake that would be their domicile for the weekend.

"Yeah, that works for me. I'll just ride with you because

Titan is going to drive up with his girl Laiya and her two cousins." Tyus informed.

"Her two cousins? Not Bianca and Shay." King's brow furrowed. "I hope Titan ain't trying to play matchmaker and shit. I was not feeling Bianca months ago and I'm not feeling her now."

"Man, you know Laiya probably put Titan up to it. He'll do whatever that girl says." Tyus paused. "But dawg, Bianca is feeling you, man. She's fine as fuck, maybe you need to try that shit again." He teased.

"Nah, I'm good. I'm real cool on her dawg. Bianca is fine - I can't deny that, but she was ready to put her ass on a platter ten minutes after we met. I don't like chicks like that, dawg."

"So, speaking of chicks you like, what's up with your girl Syncere, is she coming? Or better yet, did your, *I'm taking it slow* ass invite her?" Tyus bantered.

"Man, fuck you, dawg. I didn't get a chance to earlier." King sexily beamed reminiscing on his morning with Syncere. "I'll talk to her at some point tonight, but she'll be there." He chuckled as he playfully tussled with Zeus.

"She better man or you will be dealing with Bianca's ass all weekend. But let me answer this other call. I'll holla at you, man." Tyus disconnected the call as King footed across his bedroom into the massive closet to change his clothes and get comfortable. He checked his phone again, still no word from Syncere.

Syncere awakened on the couch with her journal and pen resting on her chest. Checking the clock, it was after 8 pm, she had no clue how long she'd been asleep. Syncere checked her messages, seeing that Symphony sent her a random meme. She noticed King's name on the text message list and reread his earlier message. *I have a proposition.* Syncere was curious about his proposition, but she also desired the soothing chords of his voice. She decided to text him first to see if he was available. Checking her phone for a response three times in sixty seconds was just plain silly, so Syncere decided to busy herself, padding to the kitchen to fill her jug with water. Her phone illuminated from across the room and Syncere darted out of the kitchen, giggling at her silliness.

King: Hey Princess. I thought you forgot about me. I'm never too busy for you. Call me whenever you're ready.

Syncere pondered multiple scenarios. *If I call right away I'll look desperate. If I text him back that will look stupid since he asked me to call.*

"Get it together Syncere." She slapped a palm to the center of her forehead. "Ok. I'll just call. This man did just have all of your ass clutched in his hands." She chuckled, pressing the button to call him.

"Hey, Princess." King's voice immediately produced a smile on her face.

"Hey, King."

"How was your appointment?" He queried.

"It was good. A clean bill of health. How was the rest of your day?"

"Hmmm, that's a loaded question." King chortled. "Let's just say I had a lot on my mind."

"Work keeping you busy?" She coyly probed, knowing exactly what he was referring to.

"Work, among other things. But I'll get those taken care of soon." King declared.

"Soon? Sounds like you have a master plan." Syncere cuddled up on her couch, grinning.

"I do, but I need your assistance for my plan to work." King was gleaming as well, sitting on the ottoman at the foot of his bed.

"Me?" She paused, pointing a finger to her chest. "What can I do to help you, King?"

"Go away with me this weekend." King blurted.

What the hell! "What? Go away with you? King, I don't know -"

"Just to Brighton. Just for the weekend, Princess." He disrupted her opportunity to resist. "My boy Tyus and his twin brother are celebrating their birthday this weekend at my

family's lake house. I would really love for you to be my guest. You would have your own room and you can bring Symphony if that makes you more comfortable." He paused. "Will you join me, Princess?"

Syncere mulled over her response for what felt like a life-time, but King remained patient, comfortable with the silence. She wanted to trust her intuition and the feelings she had for King, but Syncere was terrified of being out of control, and more importantly, hurt. She mused over Dr. Jacky's words, *open your heart, Syncere.*

"Um, let me check with Symphony. If she can go, I'll go." Syncere speedily blurted out the words before she lost her nerve.

"Excellent!" King's enthusiastic grin could be heard through the phone.

"Don't get excited. I said, *if* Symphony can go, I'll go."

"I'm not worried, Princess. Pack comfortable clothes and swimming suits. And yes, you're riding with me. I'll pick you all up on Friday around 2 pm." King confidently assured. Little did Syncere know, King had a spy, a client that worked at the hospital who already verified that her cousin wasn't scheduled to work this weekend. King didn't know Symphony well, but he did know that she was open to having a good time.

Syncere attempted to probe his confident assurance but she acquiesced. She began to realize it was pointless to argue with King when he was unwavering, resolute - determined. They talked until after midnight about nothing and everything but never discussed their morning rendezvous. Reluctant to conclude the call, they both intermittently nodded asleep until King's guttural melody soothed. "Princess, you should get some sleep. Sweet dreams, beautiful." Syncere did just that, she delighted in another night of tranquility.

7

Symphony was all too enthusiastic to spend the weekend in Brighton Falls. Syncere was barely able to ask the question before her cousin hurriedly agreed. The cousins spent Thursday afternoon with their G-ma since they would be gone for the weekend. G-ma was more excited than her favorite girls about their trip.

"What is the man's name again? King?" G-ma questioned. "He sounds wonderful."

"G-ma, why does he sound wonderful? You've never seen the man." Syncere chuckled.

"Girl, with a name like King, he's gotta be a good man." G-ma giggled. "And Symphony showed me his picture on that Instaface thing."

"Prima!" Syncere shouted, darting an evil eye in Symphony's direction.

"G-ma, I'm gonna stop telling you stuff. You can't keep secrets anymore." Symphony whispered. "Prima, I'm sorry. I kept saying how fine King is and G-ma thought I was exaggerating so I had to prove her wrong."

"So was Prima right, G-ma?" Syncere curiously probed.

"Oh yes, girly girl. He is fine and black as night. I love a dark man. You know they say, 'the darker the berry the sweeter the juice.'" G-ma cackled.

"Oooh, G-ma! You are a mess and I love it." Symphony slapped hands with her grandmother.

Syncere observed the two most important people in her life laughing at her expense as she tried to contain the roaring guffaw building in her belly. "I cannot with you two. You are both a mess...and *I* love it!" Their unison laughter echoed down the hallway.

"G-ma, call us if you need anything. The assistant has our numbers and the number to the house we're staying in. Justin's mom, Ms. Ella said she would come by to check on you Saturday, ok. We'll be back Sunday." Syncere instructed.

"I will be fine, Syncere. Ella already called me. She's bringing me some barbeque and we'll probably play bingo. Y'all don't worry about G-ma. Go and have some fun."

Syncere and Symphony had never taken a trip together, leaving their grandmother alone really since their grandfather died and definitely not since her first stroke. They were a little nervous but thankful that Ms. Ella and Justin were like family and nearby just in case. The cousins said their goodbyes to their grandmother before checking with the assistant to ensure she had all of G-ma's emergency contacts.

The cousins had appointments at the local salon Vivre III. They stopped by Syncere's apartment to drop off Symphony's luggage before walking the block to the salon.

Syncere had her twists refreshed while Symphony got waist-length cornrows. Salon manager and stylist Deeny observed as the cousins admired her work, primping in the full-length mirror.

"What are y'all up to this weekend?" Deeny questioned.

"We're going to Brighton for the weekend, so I need these braids, girl. I'm going to swim all day like a damn fish." Symphony giggled, still admiring the intricate braid pattern.

"That sounds fun. I haven't been to Brighton in years. Why didn't I get an invite to the girls' trip?" Deeny inquired.

"Girl, I'm Syncere's third wheel, so my ass barely got an invite." Symphony laughed.

"Oh shit. Wait a minute. Um, Miss Syncere? Who invited you to Brighton? I think I can take a guess though." Deeny teased.

"Take a guess then Deeny since you know so much. I'm listening." Syncere put her hand up to her ear.

Symphony jumped up and down clapping her hands. "Oh, oh, let's play a guessing game. The categories are *fine as fuck, fine and more fine, and damn he fine.*"

"I'll take *damn he fine* for $1000 Alex." Deeny snickered.

"He's a tall drink of dark chocolate milk with beautifully ripped arms and deliciously muscly thighs?" Symphony giggled as Syncere shook her head at the foolishness.

"Who is King mutherfucking Cartwright?" Deeny's raspy voice vibrated through the salon. "Yeeesss, bitch! You're finally coming to your senses. You and Nia, get on my damn nerves. She almost let that fine ass, yella ass Garrett get away and you were about to let King's ass slip through your fingers." Nia was the owner of Vivre Salons and Deeny's best friend. Nia and Garrett got engaged over Christmas in Paris, but not without a little drama from Nia.

"Deeny, it's just a trip to Brighton. He ain't taking me to Paris and I'm not marrying the man." Syncere whispered since salon patrons were now curious about the commotion. "Me and King are just friends." She bashfully smiled, recollecting the way his smooth lips felt against her skin.

Symphony and Deeny peered at each other, then at Syncere.

"Girl bye!" Symphony squealed.

"Friends my ass." Deeny chimed.

"You know what? I'm leaving." Syncere giggled. "Goodnight heffas. Prima, bring me some food if you get something." Syncere walked back to her apartment beaming at the thought of being more than just friends with King when her phone chimed.

King: Hey Princess. I'm looking forward to this weekend. Sweet dreams if I don't talk to you tonight.

Syncere blushed, anticipative, enthusiastic - and scared as shit about what the weekend would bring.

KING ARRIVED at exactly two o'clock to pick up the cousins. Syncere had already secured her apartment and decided to do a little work in the office while she waited for King.

"Prima, you're always working. Relax a little. We are

trying to have fun this weekend." Symphony encouraged, standing in the doorway of Syncere's office.

"Well, if somebody didn't ask for Gucci on their birthday and Yves Saint Laurent for Christmas, maybe I wouldn't need to work so much." Syncere cocked her head to the side, leering at her cousin.

"Oh! Well shit, please proceed. Let me not disturb you." Symphony exited the office laughing.

Minutes later, Ms. Ella's voice blared through the phone speaker, informing Syncere of King's arrival. Syncere had been a ball of nerves all morning. She was extremely anxious about spending the weekend with King, although seven other people would be there, she was still a little tense. *What are his expectations? Shit, what are my expectations? Is he going to try to finish what we started earlier this week? Do I want to finish?* Syncere ruminated.

"Hey, Princess. Are you ready to go? You look like you're deep in thought." King graced the doorway. He was a glorious sight in all white, literally stealing her breath away.

"Hi, King. I was just finalizing a few contracts before we left." Syncere smiled, standing from her office chair, giving him a glimpse of her coral spaghetti strap maxi dress. King was now breathless, noticing a second single-winged tattoo on her left shoulder, matching the one on her right.

"Superstar. Always working." King extended his hand, pulling her into a tender hug. He made it a habit to inhale her, digesting her scent - lavender and vanilla was today's flavor and he was famished and ready to feast.

Tyus was loading the truck as Syncere and King exited the office. "Tyus, this is Syncere James and her cousin

Symphony James." King introduced. "Ladies, this is my boy Tyus Okoro."

Symphony stepped in front of King, making herself known. "Hi, Tyus. I'm Symphony. I heard it's your birthday - and that there's two of you." Symphony flirtatiously extended her hand to formally introduce herself.

"Hello, gorgeous. There is only one Tyus, sweetpea." He winked and Symphony's treasure quivered.

Syncere and King rolled their eyes at the flirt fest unfolding. Shaking her head at her cousin's boldness, Syncere followed Symphony, taking a seat in the back of the truck.

"Princess, what are you doing?" King inquired.

"Um, I'm getting in the car, King. What does it look like I'm doing?"

"Seriously Princess? Can you find your way to this front seat please?" King stood at the front passenger side door, waiting for her to exit the backseat.

"I just figured Tyus would sit upfront with you - " Syncere battled.

"I think you heard the man, Prima." Symphony loudly interjected before dropping her tone to a whisper through clenched teeth, only for Syncere's ears. "Bitch, get your ass in the damn front seat."

Syncere reluctantly followed directions, taking a seat next to King. He set the GPS, checked for secured seatbelts, prayed for traveling mercy, and drove off heading towards the highway. The two-hour drive was surprisingly fun with the sounds of the '90s and early 2000's R&B and hip hop blaring through the speakers. The four of them sang and danced in their seats, making the time expire quickly.

The white Escalade pulled into the double driveway aside a black Yukon. Titan, Tyus' twin brother, had already arrived. King and Tyus opened the doors for the ladies, helping them exit the truck. Syncere and Symphony admired the expansive white lake house with black shutters, a wraparound porch with rocking chairs.

"It's beautiful, King. This is your family's house?" Syncere's orbs continued to examine the stunning home.

"Yep, I spent a lot of summers here. Come on, let me show you the house, Princess."

King escorted Syncere into the house followed by Symphony and Tyus. They entered the foyer and Syncere's breath was snatched away again in awe of the massive wooden staircase, marble floors, and crystal chandelier. The eight-bedroom house was beautifully decorated with plush white furniture accented with earthy hues of ivory, yellow, and blue. Syncere thought her bay window was huge, it paled in comparison to the colossal, six-panel patio door that fully collapsed into the wall, allowing a spectacular view of the lake.

"What's up, bro? What's up King?" A bass-filled voice resounded, shaking Syncere from her daze. "Man, this house is dope as fuck. You came through King. Thanks, man."

"What's up Titan? I'm glad you like it, dawg." King dapped the tall caramel-colored figure that mirrored Tyus, the only distinguishing feature was his beard versus Tyus' goatee.

"Did your ass steal the biggest room, Titan? I know how you get down." Tyus teased.

"Nah, that nigga know betta. I don't give a damn if it's

y'all's birthday, it's *my house* so that master bedroom is mine." King declared as the men heartily laughed. "Oh, my bad." King continued. "Titan, this is Syncere James and her cousin Symphony James."

"Hey ladies. Y'all ready to turn up this weekend?" Titan joked.

The cousins laughed and joined in on the conversation when another tall mocha specimen and three females entered the living room.

"Everybody, this is my girl Laiya, her cousins Bianca and Shay, and my boy Lennox." Titan pointed. "Y'all know Tyus and King. And this is Syncere and Symphony."

"Are y'all twins too?" Lennox quipped.

"No, we're cousins." The primas chimed in unison. Although Syncere and Symphony were ebony and ivory in skin color, many of their features were identical.

"Hi, King. It's been a long time." A dark honey-colored woman with a curly mohawk extended her arms to embrace King as he responded with a one-arm side hug.

"What's up Bianca?" King greeted, then turned towards Syncere extending his hand. "Princess, let me show you to your room."

"Princess? I thought her name was Syncere." Bianca's attempt to whisper failed.

Syncere and Symphony locked eyes, noting the suspicious exchange between King and Bianca before they followed him down the hall to a second smaller master bedroom, positioned across the hall from his, with two queen beds and ensuite bathroom.

"Does this work, ladies?" King smiled. They both nodded

in agreement. Syncere slid open the smaller patio door, stepping onto the balcony to view the lake. King followed her. "You ok, Princess?"

"I'm fine. Just taking in the beauty of this place." Syncere smiled but it didn't reach her eyes and King noticed.

"Syncere? Can you look at me?" King paused. "Are you sure you're ok? You don't like your room?"

"King, I love the room. This house, the lake, everything is just so magnificent. Like I said, just taking it all in." She shrugged, masking the little sting of jealousy she felt when Bianca hugged him.

"If you say so, pretty lady. Let me grab your bag so you can get changed. We're going to grill by the pool tonight." King positioned his sizey hands at the small of her back, kissing her forehead, and whispered. "I'm glad you're here with me."

"Me too." Her smile was brighter than the first. "I'll be ready in a little bit."

Symphony was perched on the bed as she watched King exit the room. Syncere followed behind him, closing the door.

"Now you know I'm never opposed to beating a bitch's ass." Symphony's squeaky voice vibrated. "What was that about? *It's been a long time King."* Symphony mocked Bianca's voice. "Do you think that's his ex?"

"I don't know Prima. But I refuse to believe that he would invite me knowing his ex-girlfriend would be here. I really don't want to believe that." Syncere mused aloud.

"Well, I for damn sure will find out." Symphony declared as she answered the door. "Hey King, thanks for bringing our bags. Soooo, what's up with you and Bianca?" Symphony blurted, placing a hand on her curvy hip while Syncere's eyes bulged, wishing she was invisible.

"Are you asking for a friend, a cousin, or both?" King blushingly smiled, leaning against the doorframe.

"Both!" She screeched.

Peering past Symphony, King directed his attention to Syncere who was still dumbstruck.

"Well, you can tell your cousin-friend that Bianca is not my ex anything. We've never dated, kicked it, nothing. Are we clear?" He probed.

"Ok. Whatever man. Yeah, we're clear." Symphony rolled her eyes.

"Princess, are we clear?" King posed the question to the person that he was really talking to.

"Clear." She muttered, still irritated by her cousin's intrusion.

Symphony closed the door and turned to Syncere. "There, that's settled. Let's get changed." Syncere nastily eyed her crazy ass cousin until she disappeared into the bathroom.

"Oh, so you're trying to hurt 'em, Prima!" Syncere snapped her fingers, approving her cousin's leopard print two-piece bathing suit, displaying all that James' family ass.

"Bitch, what? You're trying to kill 'em then." Symphony

grabbed Syncere's hand, spinning her around to model the shimmery black one-shoulder swimsuit with cutouts, revealing her waist and sun tattoo around her navel.

They cackled, checking their similar reflections in the mirror, and grabbed their sheer black covers before leaving the room. The cousins sashayed down the hallway into the living room.

The booming bass of the music and the roaring laughter of the house guests drew their attention to the monstrous deck. Syncere heard the distinct melodic, yet thunderous voice of King echoing from the kitchen. While Symphony joined the crowd, Syncere meandered to the kitchen to find King preparing food while rapping along with Jay-Z in the background.

She cleared her throat, trying to gain his attention to no avail. Syncere tapped him on the shoulder and he shuddered, spinning around, x-raying her from the peak of her gleaming grey orbs to the arc of her taut waist and curve of those voluptuous mahogany hips. She constantly rendered him wordless, panting, unable to capture his next breath. She was absolutely exquisite.

"Princess. You look - you are -" He stuttered. "You are stunning. Like... damn girl."

Syncere blushed, unable to contain the bashfulness she experienced with King. "Stop. Now you're making me self-conscious."

"I told you Princess; I call it like I see it." He winked.

"Can I help you with anything?" She peered around at various ingredients on the counter.

"Yes, please. Can you cut up the potatoes? The seasonings

and everything you need are in the cabinet right above you." He declared as he seasoned the steaks and salmon.

Syncere and King cooked, drank, danced, and laughed in the kitchen, happily secluded from the group. King was not shy about demonstrating his affection or attraction. Taking every opportunity to nibble, kiss, cuddle and caress her. Syncere didn't oppose. With every passing minute, she melted into King; unable to mask her allurement, she gladly accepted his tenderness. Momentarily vacating his closeness, Syncere walked down a short hallway adjacent to the kitchen into the gigantic pantry searching for the lemon juice to make lemon drop martinis.

"Hi, King." Syncere heard Bianca enter the kitchen. She delayed her exit from the pantry, shamelessly eavesdropping on the conversation.

"What's up Bianca. Tell everybody the food will be ready shortly." King blandly responded.

"So, what's up King? Are you ignoring me?" Bianca angrily questioned.

"Ignoring you? Why would I need to ignore you? You said hi, I said what's up. No more, no less." King continued moving about the kitchen as Syncere peeked from the pantry.

"Well, can I at least help you, so we can talk? Maybe get to know each other better." Bianca appeared defeated but didn't acquiesce.

"Nah, I'm good. We got it covered." King smiled, noticing Syncere's grey irises leering from the pantry door.

"We?" Bianca questioned as Syncere sashayed back into the kitchen.

"Princess, did you find what you needed?" King sexily grinned, knowing damn well Syncere was listening to the conversation.

"Yes. Thank you, King." Syncere blushed.

"Syncere, is your nickname Princess or something? Should we be calling you that?" Bianca bantered.

"No. You should not be calling me that." Syncere snapped. "Only King can call me Princess." Syncere cunningly smiled at him, demonstrating her pettiness.

"Hmm. I see. Well, looks like I'm interrupting so I'll let y'all have it then." Bianca stomped away.

"Maybe I should start calling you *petty* Princess." King guffawed, pulling Syncere into him, but she rejected his attempt.

"Nah. I wasn't being petty. It's true. Nobody can call me princess but you." Syncere pulled the salad out of the refrigerator, placing it on the island. "But um, that chick has a lot of attitude towards you for y'all not to have history." Her brow wrinkled with suspicion.

"Princess, you can just ask me about Bianca. We don't need to play games." King confidently declared.

"I'm not playing games. It's really none of my business who you've dated and/or slept with in the past. We're just friends King. So why should I be concerned?"

King deleted the gap between them, stepping in her direct path, robust arms boxing her against the island. She inhaled his cognac-laced breath, his lips pressed against her ear.

"But you *are* concerned Princess. And we both know that this is more than just a friendship." King whispered, now staring directly at her. "I know I want to be more than just your friend, Syncere."

Syncere digested his eyes, holding the gaze for what seemed like hours, but only seconds ticked by. "King. I can't - we can't talk about this right now." She ducked under his brawny arm, releasing from his trance.

King deeply exhaled, rubbing a hand down his face, refusing to observe her. "Ok, Princess. I'll keep moving at your pace. But I've made my intentions crystal clear. The ball is in your court now." King lifted the tray of meat for the grill, walking out of the kitchen, never looking back.

THE EVENING WAS RELAXING and entertaining. The food was savory, the libations were flowing, and countless cannonballs were splashed in the pool. The men resorted to playing an aggressive game of Spades while the women were tipsy off of lemon drop martinis. Bianca was quiet, other than the ludicrous eye-daggers she randomly shot at Syncere. Symphony immediately took notice and was ready for the smoke. The other ladies were pretty chill, talking and basking in the beautiful weather and strong libations.

"Syncere, girl, these lemon drops are fire." Laiya smacked her lips, delighting in the sweet and sour flavors. "I'm going to be good and drunk."

"Gone and keep drinking, baby." Titan winked at Laiya as the group loudly chuckled.

"Syncere, you work at Davenport Realty, right?" Laiya inquired as Syncere nodded. "I may need to get your information. I've been thinking about moving to Haven. I love those condos."

"Girl, you better think quick. Everything is selling fast. Grover is wide open right now though. I'll give you my information before we leave." Syncere confirmed.

"How did you get into real estate, Syncere? I guess college wasn't your thing?" Bianca spitefully probed.

"Pardon me? Why do you assume I didn't go to college?" Creased brows, both Syncere and Symphony synchronously lifted up in their lounge chairs, needing clarity quickly, while Laiya and Shay darted evil eyes at Bianca - acutely aware that she was trying to start some shit.

"I mean, you're *just* a real estate agent. That doesn't require a college degree." Bianca shrugged, peering at her cousins for agreement, but she received none.

This bitch. Symphony mused, ready to drag this chick but she knew Syncere would handle this shit without violence.

"Well, when you go to college on a full academic scholarship, graduate with a 3.9 GPA, sell over five million dollars in real estate, and manage all marketing for the number one agency in the city... I would say college was *my thing.*" Syncere rolled her eyes, taking a sip of her martini, daring Bianca to say another damn word.

King noticed some tension across the deck, with two ladies in particular. He captured Syncere's eyes, raising his brow to confirm that she was good. She nodded in confirmation. Syncere and King hadn't exchanged many pleasantries since their discord in the kitchen. They snagged glimpses of each other, King attempting to erase his somber and embittered expression, while Syncere pondered if she'd completely fucked up.

Joe's *"I Wanna Know"* blazoned through the nighttime air. King and Syncere locked eyes reminiscing about their slow dance at Melvin's. A microscopic smile formed on his lips, clearly still disappointed, but softened by the memory. Syncere's insight spoke to her in the form of her cousin.

"Bitch, you betta go get that man." Symphony's matching orbs bulged, staring at Syncere until her feet started moving.

8

Syncere nervously footed across the deck to where King and the other guys were seated. He eyeballed her from the time she stood until she reached him. Syncere gently placed a hand on his shoulder, bending to whisper in his ear. "Can you take me to the lake?"

King contemplated for half a second, striving to play hard to get, but failing miserably. He placed his hand over hers that was still caressing his shoulder. "Yeah, Princess. I got you." King rose to his feet, dressed in swim trunks and a tank top that cradled his athletic frame. Still clutching her hand, he escorted Syncere down the deck steps and opened the gate leading to a path towards the lake.

The five-minute journey down the trail to the lake was soundless - no dialogue. King felt that he'd communicated his position so it wasn't necessary for him to initiate conversation. His adoration for Syncere was unblemished, straightforward - shit, clear as fucking day. They reached a wooden bench facing the lake where they settled in silence. The luminous glow of the full moon reflected against the placid water.

"King, I'm complicated." Syncere blurted, turning to face him with dewy eyes. This was going to be a laborious conversation for her, but she gravelly desired him - and his understanding. "I've been hurt to my soul in the past, so I've created a wall - these directives, rules, agreements to guide my attachments or non-attachments with men." She paused, emotions brewing, legs trembling.

King tenderly placed his hand against her thigh to cease the tremble. " I'm a smart man, Princess. I can manage complicated things. As for these rules, I've told you before, rules are made to be broken. I would bet that you've already dishonored a few with me, am I right?"

"Yes. I have completely disregarded them with you. But that's the problem, King, I - I'm broken - shattered. I don't believe I'm capable of being what you need me to be." Syncere didn't intend to do as Dr. Jacky recommended, but she released. The torrent tears escaped her cloudy grey orbs.

King quickly canceled any space separating him from her. He closed his monstrous arms around Syncere, encouraging her to find respite in him. Syncere laid her head against his sturdy chest and slowly allowed her heart to break, for more reasons than King would ever know.

"Princess, baby, if you are broken - then you are beautifully broken in my eyes. I can't change your past hurt or in no way am I trying to fix you." He cupped her chin towards his face. "Baby, I just want to be able to mend the broken pieces and offer you new opportunities to heal - with me." King delicately kissed her forehead, her nose, and her lips. "I want you Syncere, as is."

Syncere chortled through her tears. "You make me sound like a foreclosed property with a shitty ass roof and rusted pipes."

King boisterously guffawed. "Nah, Princess. I already cherish what's right here. No upgrades, no inspections, no transformative flips necessary- you are perfect and I'm sold."

King wiped the continuous stream of tears before he conquered her pouty lips, running his fingers through her braids. Tenderly, gently, softly kissing her as he whispered, "I just want you, Princess. That's all. Just you."

Syncere's heart was fiercely pounding, she placed a hand over her heart to catch it before catapulting through her chest. Misty-eyed, she caressed his chest, journeying her hands to rub his nape, her fingers ever-so-softly massaging through his hair. King parted her lips with his substantial tongue, grazing the curves of her pretty face. He momentarily relinquished her lips as his tongue occupied her honeysuckle scented neck.

Syncere was hazy, breathing heavy, treasure drenched. Still snuggled in the folds of her neck, he easily lifted her to straddle his lap. Syncere didn't resist. King's imposing hands explored the same trail as he did that morning in her apartment. Cuddling her swollen breast, nipples distended against the shimmery fabric, he journeyed to her treasure. Kneading, fondling, palming the crown of her jewel, driving Syncere insane, he smoothly shifted the fiber of the swimsuit, unveiling her pulsating treasure. King slithered one finger, then two, in and out, and in and out of her ocean.

"Damn, Princess. You are so fucking wet. Baby, I just want to taste you." King captured her incomprehensible words and moans with his mouth, reclaiming authority of her lips. Incessantly thrusting his saturated fingers, deeper, harder, Syncere lost all sense of taste, smell, and control.

"Shit! King!" Syncere mumbled against his lips. "What are you-what are doing to me?"

Not breaking the rhythmic stride of his fingers, his only response, "Come for me, Princess." Goosebumps surfaced as her body started to quake and tremble, ears popping and eyes cloudy, as she rode every delightful stroke, tears still streaming down her face.

"Aah! King!" Syncere's moan echoed in the midnight breeze. He gently released his fingers, teasing her treasure causing a literal and figurative flood. Syncere shuddered, practically collapsing against his body, her face buried in his cocoa-colored neck.

King trailed his fingers up and down her back, soothing the salacious sting. "Are you ok Princess?" She was tongue-less - zero words. "Syncere? Baby, you good?" He stroked her face, encouraging her to look at him.

"Mmmhmm. Yes, I'm ok. I'm good, King." Syncere felt dizzy, faint, disoriented. *If he can do all that with just his fingers, I don't think I'm ready for that monster pressing against his shorts.* Syncere tried not to stare as she slowly lifted from his heated frame, repositioning herself on the wooden bench.

"Are *we* good?" King pointed a finger between them. "I meant what I said, Syncere. I will go at whatever pace you prefer. This sounds crazy after what just happened, but I don't want to rush you."

"Shhh." She placed a finger over his lips. "It wouldn't have happened if I didn't want it to happen, King. I promise you, we're good. Ok?"

"I hear you. Let's head back to the house." Syncere nodded as King stood, pulling her to join him. They leisurely strolled back to the lake house, hands clasped, beaming faces, dreamy orbs.

———————

"HOW WAS THE LAKE PRIMA?" Symphony squealed while she and Tyus were a little too cuddly in the pool.

"It was good Prima. Thank you for asking." Syncere teased.

"I can't keep up with all of these damn nicknames - Princess, Prima. What the hell?" Bianca blurted.

"And I don't recall anybody asking your ass too!" Symphony shouted from the pool. She turned to Tyus, not attempting to mute. "I'm about two seconds off that bitch. She didn't think I heard her talking all that shit when King and Syncere left."

"Bitch?" Bianca yelled. "Girl, you betta gone with that."

"Or what?" Symphony started exiting the pool as Tyus grabbed her.

"Aye, aye. Y'all not getting ready to do that shit up in my house." King shouted. "Bianca, if you have a problem, we'll find a way for you to get home. If you're ready to chill with that shit, then you can stay. Symphony - calm the hell down, girl."

Syncere knelt next to the pool trying to quell her cousin. Symphony was like a pit bull, always ready to attack and win. Tyus ensured Syncere that he would keep an eye on Symphony as King walked to the pool to retrieve his princess.

"Symphony? Man, don't let that girl fuck up your weekend. She's on some bullshit." King declared.

"Titan invited her, so he's gonna handle that shit, King. I got lil Symphony Mayweather over here." He joked. "She's going to be cool. Ain't that right, sweetpea?" Tyus winked.

King and Syncere peered at each other, furrowed brows, bewildered by what was going on before their eyes. "Yeah, um, that's our queue to exit immediately." King teased as he and Syncere cackled. He wrapped an arm around her shoulders, leading her to the other side of the wraparound porch.

Although their view of the lake was obstructed by the houses and trees, they relaxed on the oversize outdoor couch, still covered by the full moon. King and Syncere talked, laughed, kissed, and cuddled until they both drifted to sleep.

"No. Dav-. Please. Nnn-. Please." Syncere's words were low and muffled but her body thrashed and flailed enough to awaken King.

"Princess. Baby. Wakeup." He gently shook her. Syncere shivered, eyes narrowed until she comprehended her surroundings. "Princess, you were having a bad dream. Are you ok?" King lightly brushed back the loose braids that grazed her cheek.

"I'm fine. I'm ok. Just a crazy dream." She inhaled and exhaled deeply, attempting to gain composure.

"Look at me, Princess. Are you really fine? Syncere, you can talk to me." King assured.

"King, I promise. I'm good. Can we go in the house? It's getting chilly." Syncere swiftly dismounted the couch with King following behind her.

They entered the house, slowly ambling down the hallway as King walked her to her room. Syncere peeked in, noticing Symphony was nowhere to be found. She was hoping her cousin would be in the room so they could talk until the unpleasant memories vanished. Still visibly trembling from both the nightmare and the night's chill, Syncere crossed her arms over her body for warmth.

"Syncere, you are still shaking. Baby, you can talk to me. Can you please tell me what's going on?" King begged.

"King. I'm fine. It was a crazy dream. I don't even remember. So just let it go, please." Glossy eyes silently pleading with him.

"Ok. I'll let it go for now." King stared, reading her frightened eyes. "Princess, do you want to be alone tonight?" He questioned, stroking the tip of her nose.

Syncere paused momentarily, captivated by his authentic desire to protect her. "No," Syncere whispered.

———————————

KING LEANED against the doorway as he watched her gather what she needed from her room. He was troubled, anxious - concerned about her. His gut told him there was more to the story. King couldn't decipher much of what she was saying in her sleep, but she was helpless, petrified. Syncere reappeared in the door, breaking his daze.

King escorted her across the hall to his room, where she took a shower, washing away the good and bad of the day. She lotioned with honeysuckle body butter and dressed in purple pajama shorts and a matching tank top before exiting the bathroom. Their favorite R&B jams whispered in the background while King nodded off to sleep waiting for Syncere until he smelled her delicious scent tickle his nose.

King footed across the room crossing paths with her as he headed to the bathroom. He tugged at her waist pulling Syncere into a protective hug, inhaling the tantalizing fragrance simmering from her flesh. Concern still invading his spirit. King showered while Syncere was restless, tussling in the silky white sheets until she decided to navigate to Dr. Jacky's website to read the affirmations. *I am not responsible for something I did not consent to. I can create a safe space for myself.* She continually repeated until King entered the room.

"I thought you would be asleep, Princess." King was beautiful. That's the only way she could describe him. His gooey-butter skin glistened against the black shorts and white tank.

"No, not yet. A little restless I guess." Syncere tossed her loose braids over her shoulder, repositioning in the California king bed to face him.

"Baby, come here." King extended his arm, beckoning her to lay against his chest. She obliged.

Syncere loved when he called her princess, but hearing King refer to her as 'baby,' ignited a thunderous flood in her treasure. "I guess Bianca needs to add *'baby'* to her list of names to remember." Syncere giggled.

"Petty Princess." King sang as they laughed. "But seriously, Princess, I don't know what's going on with you and I won't pry. I just hope you'll tell me when you're ready." He paused, adjusting her head to connect with his eyes. "But in the meantime, will you let me help you fall asleep?"

"How do you plan on doing that, King?" She blushed.

"You ask a lot of questions for someone who said they trust me. So, I'll ask you again, can I put you to sleep tonight, Princess?" Syncere nodded. "Baby, I need to hear you say the word." King requested.

"Yes." She whimpered.

King could smell the entanglement of honeysuckle lotion and the sugared nectar of Syncere's treasure. He was wasted, hammered, disorderly, completely intoxicated by her scent - drunk in love. Syncere was panting, quivering with anticipation. Her mind had her ready to run for cover while her treasure was enthusiastically willing to oblige. King was teasing her, sucking, nibbling, and biting everywhere but where she needed - shit, wanted him to be.

King dismantled every rule, destroyed every barrier with his tender gestures and sweet kisses. Syncere's protective wall was becoming just as imaginary and insane as Donald Trump's. King sweetly kissed as he disrobed her, unveiling her mahogany flesh - beautifully exhibited for his viewing pleasure.

King laid her gently on her back, hovering, focused on those captivating grey eyes he treasured. He kissed her forehead, nose, lips, and continued his explorer-ship down her quivering flesh until his mouth met the crown of her jewel. King lounged there for a moment, deeply inhaling the flavorful aroma, his steaming breath sent a blissful chill up her spine.

"Princess, relax, I promise I'll take care of you," King whispered against the folds of her pulsating private lips. Seconds later, his heated mouth tongue-kissed her sweltering treasure, twisting, turning, licking to the rhythm and blues beats drumming in the background.

"Princess, you're so damn sweet." He delighted in her mouthwatering juices.

"Aahh! King!" Syncere moaned, fisting the sheets, back arched, and grabbing for anything to rescue her from the lustful tongue lashing. She earnestly strived to retreat because she knew her death was inevitable - anything that felt that good had to be deadly. Syncere couldn't formulate a coherent sentence. "King. Shit. Baby." King firmly gripped her thighs, preventing escape, never coming up for air until — "Oh my God, King!" Syncere's climactic whimper played a beautiful melody. She couldn't breathe, joyfully hyperventilating - she was about to die the most euphoric death.

King moved stealthily up the length of her body like a black panther hunting prey while kissing every tremble and goosebump with his treasure-flavored lips. He floated above her, digesting her beauty, reconciling what was about to happen. Syncere was flushed, labored breathing, overwhelmed by King's care, allure, and adoration, yet still anxious. His thunderous timbre broke her gaze.

"Whatever happened in the past.... Whatever he did... I promise I will never hurt you, Syncere." King could never comprehend the magnitude of his words. Syncere felt free, graciously consenting to his soft, gentle, deliberate strokes as he inhabited her. Massaging the walls of her saturated treasure, inch by glorious inch. Thick, heavy, veiny and so fucking good.

"Princess! You feel like heaven. Shit. You're everything I imagined." King was fighting to control his animalistic nature. He wanted to act hastily, devour her, but he had to be delicate, slowly dismantling her complicated layers with every stroke.

Persistently, meticulously thrusting at the most tantalizing tempo, her treasure uniting with his girthy command, her inhale indistinguishable from his exhale. The weightiness of King's penetration grew deeper, more intense. Syncere's body broadcasted an unfamiliar response, something she'd never experienced before - quaking, trembling, convulsing, shit, insanely out of control. She joyously screamed his name "King," lacking any concern of being heard. Her gratification grew louder, "KING," as a torrent resounding moan escaped him and they simultaneously reached the pinnacle, a glorious give and take, fulfilling a magnificently mind-blowing climax.

9

The late Sunday morning in Brighton was radiant, peaceful, and breathtaking with the sun beaming through the French doors of the master bedroom suite. Syncere awakened clothed in nothing but King's protective arms for the second morning. They'd spent the past two nights entangled in fiercely passionate lovemaking until Syncere would literally blackout, waking up discombobulated, yet completely satisfied.

Syncere and King spent Saturday on his family's boat on the lake with the rest of the group. It was apparent to onlookers that Syncere and King's relationship had escalated to another level. They could not be contained - openly flirting, kissing, hugging, caressing.

The group was packing and getting ready to head back home but made a stop for brunch at the Toussaint Family Winery & Distillery owned by King's college friend Nicolas Toussaint and his sister Naomi. King was excited to show Syncere the winery because he knew how much she appreciated beautiful things. If she was in awe of the lakehouse, she would fall in love with the gorgeous historic architecture the winery offered.

Syncere was glowing in the yellow strapless floor-length sundress as she stood on the patio overlooking the vineyard. King literally could not take his eyes off of her, afraid that with any delayed blink he would awake from his dream and she would be gone. But it wasn't a hallucination, it was genuine and she was real.

"Damn King. You are staring at her as if she's going to vanish. Y'all was just all over each other." Titan teased.

"I know that look. It's the look of satisfaction. King had a taste of the lovely Syncere and now this nigga acting like a man in love." Tyus bantered.

"Maybe I am." King's eyes momentarily diverted from his pleasing perusal of Syncere to leer at his friends. "As a matter of fact, I am absolutely *in love* with Syncere."

"Aww shit. She got you sprung dawg. Does she know you're in love?" Lennox decided to chime in.

"Not yet, but she will." King connected eyes with Syncere, exchanging a sexy smile.

"Damn dawg, do I need to book the winery for a summer wedding?" Nicolas quipped, joining in on the group guffaw but noticed King wasn't laughing. "King, man, you're serious?"

"I don't think I've ever been more serious about anything in my life, man. I am so in love with that woman, but Princess is delicate. I have to be gradual, move at her pace." King crooked his pointer finger, beckoning her to come to him as he rose to meet her halfway.

King vowed to keep his word, to not be hasty, but he couldn't deny his feelings. He was in love with Syncere and would not be able to withhold his devotion and adoration for long.

"What do you think Princess?" He pressed his lips to her forehead.

"It's absolutely stunning and the food was delicious. I can't believe I've never heard of this place. I clearly need to get out of Haven more." Syncere giggled as she cuddled into him. Her unprompted display of affection was continuing to amaze them both. Any public display of any kind with a man was foreign to Syncere, so the fact that she craved to be close to King in every moment was startling.

"We can come back whenever you desire, Princess." King blushed.

"Bet?" She tossed up her fist, smile beaming and eyes sparkling.

"Bet." He agreed, fist-bumping her and sealing his promise with a kiss.

The ride back to the city was just as eventful as the drive to Brighton. King pulled in front of Syncere's apartment a little after 7 pm. The packed weekend left everyone exhausted, but King and Syncere were reluctant to separate. They'd comforted each other for the past two nights and craved more. Tyus walked Symphony to her car parked behind the building while King walked Syncere to her apartment.

"I can stay." King blurted as soon as he crossed the threshold, pulling Syncere against his chest.

"King, we both have busy days tomorrow and you have to get ready for Chicago right?"

Syncere desperately wanted him to stay but also needed to process the events of the weekend alone.

"All the more reason for me to stay, Princess." He nestled into the folds of her neck.

"Who's going to fight old ladies to get your croissants while I'm gone?" He joked.

"I think I can manage, King." She winked.

"If you say so." He paused. "Will you have dinner with me when I get back on Friday? I'll make sure to have all of the surprises you hate."

"Yes, I would love dinner but no more surprises." Syncere nudged him towards the front door. "King, thank you for a spectacular weekend."

"It was my pleasure, Princess." King's intense gaze said so much more than his words.

He caressed the curves of her face leaving her breathless from the sensuous kiss.

SYNCERE BUSIED herself all week trying not to think about missing King. She didn't think his absence in the office would impact her, but it did. Syncere and King connected briefly on

Monday afternoon before his evening flight to Chicago, but the atmosphere was different without him filling the space. Syncere was greeted daily by a special delivery of roses, candy, cards, just about everything King could ponder to ensure he occupied her mind. They'd text throughout the day and talk all night until Syncere fell asleep, slumbering through the night.

"Hey, Princess. How was your day?" King returned to his hotel after a grueling day of meetings at multiple construction sites.

"It was good - busy. How about you? You sound tired." Syncere unsuccessfully attempted to minimize the grin on her face.

"I am. I'm exhausted. I toured the first site at 6 am and have been going since then." He yawned.

"King, get some rest. You'll be back tomorrow. We can talk then." She insisted.

"What are you doing right now?" King detoured the conversation.

"Don't try to change the subject. You heard me. Get some rest, King."

"Alright, babe. Peaceful dreams Princess. I –" He paused, pondering the potential implications of his words that were ready to flow so freely.

"You what? What were you about to say?" Syncere probed.

"I just miss you, Princess. That's all." King estimated that Syncere wasn't ready for what he wanted to share.

"I - I miss you too." Syncere stuttered, still self-conscious about being so forthcoming with her feelings.

They said goodnight with King crashing as soon as they

disconnected. It was a little too early for Syncere so she pulled a few home listings for some clients, did a little online retail therapy, and watched the movie "Just Wright" as if it was her first time until she retired to the bed.

———————

"I - I can't breathe. Davis, please. Please don't do this." Hysterical, panicking, savagely screaming.

"Stop fighting Syncere, just let it happen, baby. I promise I'll make you want to come back for more." Breathe scorching, harmful, firm hands.

"Davis! No. Please stop. You're hurting me. Oh God, please help me. I can't breathe. Please, don't do this. Davis. No!"

"Prima! Oh my God! What the fuck happened to your face? Who did this to you? Did Davis do this? I will kill that mutherfucker."

"Davis raped me, Dean Jacobs, and you're asking about what clothes I was wearing. This is bullshit. Why don't you believe me?"

Click. Click. Click. "How many pictures do you have to take? I just want to put my clothes on."

"No. I'm not on birth control."

"Please, don't do this. Davis. No!"

Syncere awakened in a frenzy. Fighting, kicking, screaming, panting, she could not breathe. Multiple tormenting flashbacks played on repeat in her head. The firmness of his sweaty hands, the scent of his cologne filtrating the air felt real. Images of Davis' dangerously crude smirk as he slapped her circulated throughout the room. She ran from the counterfeit images, shuffling to the top of the bed, balled in the fetal position, trembling.

Sweat running from her brow, pajamas drenched. She tasted blood on her tongue. Recalling the wobbly walk home after, she grabbed her purse from his car and ran. Vividly recollecting Symphony's reaction when she saw Syncere's face. The meaningless call to campus police. The pictures of her bruises that mysteriously disappeared. The visit to Planned Parenthood, but it was too late.

Syncere picked up her phone glaring at the date. September 27th, ten years since her life was turned topsy-turvy. The lucid nightmare completely crippled her. Her body was physically responsive to the trauma as if it happened yesterday. Syncere was visibly trembling as she padded into her bathroom, praying a steamy shower would wash away the treacherous memories. The fiery water spilled down her face mixing with her tears.

Syncere was still quaking as she exited the shower. She wrapped her terrified spirit into a plush white robe, footing into her kitchen to brew peppermint tea, water still dripping from her saturated braids. Nothing was working. She contemplated calling Dr. Jacky, but her shaky hands couldn't hold the phone. Syncere shuddered, dropping the phone, frightened by the sound. *Symphony. I can't talk to her right now.* She mused.

"Syncere, get your shit together." She exhaled deeply before reciting her affirmations. "I am not responsible for something I did not consent to. I can create a safe space for myself." Still no relief. *It's not working.* She silently cried.

Syncere peered at her hands still vibrating, her skin was clammy, piercing sensations shooting through her feet, the right side of her head throbbing and heart palpitating. She was having a panic attack. Syncere pulled the curtains closed, darkening the living room. She perched in her bay window continually reciting her affirmations, praying, while rocking back and forth. Syncere continued to tremble until she passed out in the bay window.

Hours later, Syncere leaped from the window seat, blinking to focus her blurred vision. She stared at the large clock against her living room wall until the time became clear- it was three o'clock. Syncere had no idea how long she'd been out but her head was still pounding. Her phone illuminated, missed calls from G-ma and text messages from Symphony, King, Justin, and Ms. Ella.

Ms. Ella: Syncere, where are you? Your clients are here.

Justin: Syn. What's going on girl? We were supposed to be meeting today and you had clients. Call me.

Prima: Prima, you ok today? I know it's going to be hard but you're in such a good place. I love you.

King: Princess, are you ok? I've called and text all morning. I'm worried. My flight lands at 2:35. Call me.

Syncere stared at her phone for what felt like a lifetime. She pondered calling Symphony but she didn't want to disturb her at work and King was probably still inflight. Syncere was certain that King's warmth and firm embrace would help her through this episode. The trembles and flashbacks would cease. But what would she tell him? The truth? Would he believe her?

King's flight landed a little early and he still couldn't

reach Syncere. He fought through the crowded airport, sprinting to valet to retrieve his car. King jumped in his Escalade, desperately needing to find Syncere. He continued to call, text, and even contacted Symphony but still no clear explanation for Syncere's absence. King pulled in front of the realty office, Justin and Ms. Ella was concerned - still no sign of his princess.

The thunderous banging against her door shook Syncere from her daze.

"Princess, are you in there? Please say something, Syncere. I know you're here; I saw your car." He paused. "Baby, please. Are you ok? Syncere?" He yelled as he continued banging. "I talked to Symphony, she said you were having a rough day but wouldn't tell me why. Baby, let me help you, please."

Syncere's beautiful grey eyes were placid, painfully reddened. She was numb, dizzy, and all cried out. Syncere aimlessly shuffled across the room, unlocking the door, but didn't turn the knob to open it. She meaninglessly wandered back to the seated bay window, zombiesque, robe loosely disheveled as King slowly entered her apartment. The room was dusky, the curtains blocked any potential ray of sunlight. King tugged the curtain, allowing a glimpse of sunshine, then gingerly approached her. She was void of the smile he adored, her glistening grey orbs cloudy.

"Princess. Baby, are you ok?" He whispered, standing near the window, careful not to startle her.

Syncere was hushed, eyes dilated, not focused. She slowly shook her head - she was not ok.

"Did something happen to you? Did somebody hurt

you?" King angrily questioned. "Princess, can I sit with you, here in the window?"

She nodded, giving her permission for him to sit.

"Baby, what happened?" He carefully settled on the cushioned window seat. King furrowed with confusion and concern.

"I was raped," Syncere interjected, her monotone voice at a whisper. "Ten years ago, today. I was a junior in college. The happiest time of my life. And he - he stole that from me." Eyes fixed, tears unleashed. "I can still smell him - feel the slap against my face - the blood on my lips. It's been ten years and it feels like it just happened today. That's crazy. I sound crazy, right?" Her eyes finally met his.

"No, Princess. It's not crazy. You're not crazy." King didn't probe. He just listened.

"It was like he planned it. He pursued me for weeks. The date, his roommate losing his key, getting me to his apartment. It was all a part of his plan." Syncere curled up tighter, hugging her knees into her chest. "But it wasn't my fault. I know that now. It didn't matter what I was wearing. It wasn't my fault." She swayed, threatening to fall off of the seat. "I fought him. I kicked, screamed. I said no. But they didn't believe me. They all lied. Covered it up." The vehement sobs stained her face. King slowly closed the distance between them, prepared to catch her if she fell.

"Syncere, I believe you." He paused. "Baby, can I come closer?"

She nodded, collapsing into King's arms, releasing a scream that echoed through the ceiling. King picked her up, carrying Syncere to the bedroom where he gently settled her on the bed as she continued to wail. Her bedroom was dark as he navigated his way to the bathroom. King warmed a towel, placing it against her brow.

"Syncere, can I hold you?" He whispered.

"Yes. Please." She confidently affirmed through her tears.

King encased her, caressing until she calmed. With her permission, he removed the sweat-drenched robe after reheating the towel to cleanse her body. King wiped Syncere's flushed skin from head to toe, draping her with the silken sheets until she was ready to get dressed. Syncere observed King, narrowly eying his every move as he delicately cared for her.

"King? Can you just lay with me? Please?" She requested and he obliged.

He pressed his chest firmly against her back, cradling her in his Herculean frame. King inhaled her honey scent, softly kissing her face, whispering, "Baby I got you. I won't let anybody hurt you." He consoled her until her tears ceased.

"What have you eaten?" He probed.

"I had some tea. I'm not hungry." She whined.

"Syncere, you're going to make yourself sick. You need to eat babe."

"King, I'm fine." She stressed.

"You have to eat. I have food coming. Will you try to eat something? For me, please."

"For you, I'll try." She paused. "King, there is something else I need to tell you."

"Syncere, you don't have to tell me anything else. Baby, you've said enough." The thought of her trauma infuriated

King. He didn't ask for the name of her rapist, but he was certain he would kill whoever hurt her.

"I got pregnant...from the rape." She blurted. "I had a baby. A girl. Her name is Mariah." Syncere exhaled. "The scar, the infinity tattoo - that's from her." She turned her body, tightly cuddling King's massive chest. "My butterfly tattoos, I got them after she was born - we are separated like the butterfly wings, but always together." Syncere smiled. "She was adopted by a great family. I just couldn't - I couldn't raise his child." She glared at King. "Does that make me a bad person?"

"No, Princess. It doesn't. You made the choice that was best for you and her." He rested his lips against her forehead.

"I hated my mother for basically abandoning me. I promised I would never do that to my kid, but - I did it anyway." Silent tears escaped.

"Princess, you didn't abandon her. You gave her life. And a good family. You could've made another choice, but you didn't. So that doesn't make you a bad person. It makes you extremely brave." He encouraged her.

"They - her parents, send me pictures every year. And every year they ask if I want to meet her. Every year I decline."

"May I ask why?" King whispered.

"I never want her to know the circumstances behind her conception. And I don't know if I could see her in the flesh without flashing back to him." She shrugged.

"Understood." King's phone buzzed. "Baby, that's the food. Do you feel like getting dressed while I take care of this?"

"Yeah. I'm getting up. I need to call Justin anyway."

"It's already done. I called him, Ms. Ella, and Symphony to let them know you were ok. I would've called G-ma but I don't have her number." He joked and finally got a glimpse of her beautiful smile.

King exited the bedroom while Syncere schlepped out of the bed into the bathroom. Staring at her reflection in the mirror, the puffiness subsided, her breathing normalized and the hideous images fading. She activated the music app, selecting Tasha Cobbs Leonard radio. The heavens must've been listening because the first song to play was *"Gracefully Broken."* Syncere solemnly exhaled as the words massaged her fragmented spirit. She happily sang although tears were falling. *"Here I am, God. Arms wide open. Pouring out my life. Gracefully broken."* King heard the heartbreak and redemption in her harmonious sound. He contemplated interrupting her to offer comfort, but he knew she needed this time alone. Syncere sang through several songs while dressing in a black racerback flowy dress until the tears diminished. She felt lighter, free, unrestrained.

———

THE DELECTABLE AROMA of the food tickled Syncere's senses. She was finally a little hungry. Syncere footed into the great room to find the dining room table set with candles, flowers, food, and King. He looked tasty enough to satisfy in light grey slacks, powder blue shirt rolled up at the sleeves exposing the crown tattoo on his forearm.

"Oh, my goodness. King, what is all of this?" Syncere inquired, peering at the elegantly plated food.

"It's dinner, Princess." He winked.

"I can see that it's dinner. But, Doordash didn't deliver this type of food and I wasn't in the bedroom long enough for you to cook. Where did it come from?"

"Well, I'd arranged for a chef to come to my house tonight to cook for us. But, since there was a change of plans, I asked him to prepare the food and bring it here." King extended his hand, pulling her into him for a kiss.

"King, I'm so sorry. I completely forgot about dinner. I didn't mean to ruin your plans."

"We're still having dinner together, Princess. That's all that matters to me." He stroked the bridge of her nose, guaranteed to make her gleam and it did. "Have a seat?" King pulled out her seat before taking his next to her.

"This looks delicious. I definitely think I'm hungry now." She giggled.

"Good. Are you in the mood for some wine?" King pointed to the red zinfandel before she agreed.

He prepared Syncere's plate - stuffed chicken breast, rice casserole, and grilled asparagus. He led them in prayer before they proceeded to consume the delicious meal. They engaged in conversation, and King was ecstatic to finally capture a bit of shimmer in her eyes as she laughed. Their joint laughter was interrupted by a familiar sound glaring from Syncere's phone. It was her grandmother calling. King blushed, recalling what they were doing the last time he heard that song.

"Hi, G-ma." Her grandmother could hear the smile through the phone.

"Hey, girly girl. You sound like you're feeling ok. How are you?" G-ma inquired.

"I'm fine G-ma," Syncere uttered.

"No Syncere, how are you *really* doing? You always say you're fine when you want me to leave you alone." She scolded.

"Really G-ma, I'm much better. I struggled earlier but I feel one hundred percent better now." Syncere blushed as King winked before taking a sip of his wine.

"Is Symphony with you? I don't want you to be alone tonight." G-ma was nervous and concerned about her grand-daughter. Although the panic attacks were better, she'd comforted Syncere through one too many over the past ten years.

"No. Prima is working tonight. This is her long weekend." Syncere clarified.

"Oh, that's right. I didn't pay attention to my calendar. I wish I could be there with you, baby girl. I just hate that you are alone." G-ma huffed.

"I'm not alone G-ma. Um, King is here - "

"Oh, really. Well, that's wonderful. Let me talk to him." G-ma giddily interjected.

Syncere's brow creased as she rolled her eyes baffled by her grandmother's request. *Now, why does she need to talk to him?*

"Syncere? Let me talk to him for a minute." G-ma repeated.

"Um, my grandmother wants to talk to you." Syncere

extended the phone to King; they were wearing matching masks of confusion.

"Hello. Hi. Mrs. James." King mumbled. "How are you, ma'am?"

"Well, hello, King. I am exceedingly well, praise the Lord." She giggled. "How are you, young man?"

"I am doing well. Pretty good." He smiled at Syncere; he was good because she was good.

"King, I've heard about you from my other grand-daughter Symphony. She says you think very highly of my Syncere. Is that right?" The inflection in her voice dared him to say otherwise.

"Yes ma'am. Very much so." King spoke with certainty.

"I don't know how much Syncere has shared with you, but my baby has been severely hurt in the past. Unspeakable pain." G-ma paused, clearing her throat to prevent the tears. "She's a beautiful girl - smart, thoughtful, a wonderful heart, a tough cookie. But with all of that, Syncere is fragile. Do you understand, King?"

"Yes, Mrs. James. I completely understand." King heard the sincerity, love, and heartache in G-ma's tone.

"Syncere hasn't found a man she can trust, where she feels safe. The fact that you are there right now lets me know that she trusts you and feels protected. But you mustn't rush or pressure, or she will shrink and isolate. And I can't see her go through that again. Do you understand me, young man? If you're going to be there, take her as she is, and cherish her." G-ma sniffed, the tears had released.

Syncere started cleaning the dishes while King was still on the phone. He stood, eradicating the space that kept him from her, placing one hand over hers to halt any movement, while the other held the phone. He gazed directly into her slaty orbs before responding to G-ma. "Mrs. James, I promise you that Syncere can trust me and you can trust me. I am here to protect her and cherish her if that is what Princess desires."

Syncere and G-ma's matching eyes were threatening tears. Once again, King rendered Syncere breathless and overwhelmed with emotions. G-ma took the opportunity to fill the void.

"Well, that is wonderful to hear and I will hold you to it as long as there is breath in my body." She snickered. "Let me speak to my granddaughter please."

"Hey, G-ma," Syncere whispered, still connected to King's gaze.

"Girly girl, I told you - with a name like King, his momma knew he was going to be a good man." She cackled. "I know you don't want to hear this but that man is in love. And before you refute it just listen. Don't run from love, Syncere. Just let the cards fall where they may. You are a survivor, babygirl. You can get through anything and you deserve all the love your heart can hold. You hear me?"

"Yes, ma'am. I hear you and I understand. I love you so much G-ma." Syncere finally broke away from King's onyx eyes, disconnecting the call.

"Forgive my grandmother. I can only imagine what she was saying." Syncere coyly smiled.

"She said everything that a person who loves you and wants the best for you is supposed to say." King declared as he cut slices of pineapple cheesecake. "You ready for dessert? At the table or on the couch?" He queried.

They padded over to the couch with cheesecake and more wine in tow. Syncere greedily demolished the cheesecake, giggling as she forked a piece of King's while he was in the restroom. He reappeared wearing his shoes that he removed earlier. Syncere's heart deflated a bit at the idea of him leaving. She rose, preparing to walk him to the door.

"Thanks for everything, King. I always appreciate you." Syncere said, wearing an imposter smile.

"Are you putting me out, Princess?" King questioned.

"You have on your shoes so I figured you were leaving." She shrugged.

"You are trying to get me in trouble with your G-ma." King cackled. "She made me promise that I wouldn't leave you tonight, so I'm not leaving. I was just going to get my bag from the car." He smiled. "I'm just doing what I was told. Is that ok with you, Princess?"

"Yes. I was really hoping you would stay." Syncere surprisingly confessed.

"I'll be here for however long you need me." He kissed the tip of her nose.

King changed into basketball shorts and a t-shirt after he retrieved his luggage from the car. They cuddled on the couch watching something with Kevin Hart as King's words echoed repeatedly in Syncere's dome.

She already trusted him, but Syncere wanted to probe what he meant by cherishing her. But was she ready to fully disclose her feelings for King? Does she even know how she truly feels about him?

Syncere had never loved a man before. She'd never uttered those three words to any man but her grandfather when he was alive. *Could I really be in love with King? Does he love me? Am I ready to love and to be loved?* Syncere silently mused until she fell asleep in the comfort of King's arms.

10

The warm, summer weather had been replaced by cool, fall October nights. A month had passed since Syncere's panic attack. She'd been seeing Dr. Jacky once a week and making great progress, experiencing no nightmares since that night. Syncere was extremely careful not to rely on having King around to keep her balanced, although he'd been a delightful distraction. She strived to ensure she built the muscle and leveraged the appropriate techniques and resources to effectively manage her PTSD on her own. If King had it his way, he desired to awake to her exquisite mahogany face every morning and slumber in a joint embrace every night.

King traveled to Chicago again for business while Syncere was engrossed in closing contracts for the new build community in Grover Point. Although the past few months were hectic, Syncere had already exceeded her sales quota and was preparing to launch the new marketing campaign for the commercial business once Justin solidified negotiations. Syncere hadn't been involved in the meetings with the prospective new partner since she did not conduct commercial sales, but she would present the marketing campaign during the next meeting in two weeks.

King desperately missed Syncere. He was trying to accelerate his meetings so he could take an earlier flight to surprise her. The past couple of months with her had been laborious, yet fascinating. Syncere didn't lie, she was extremely complicated. King had a better understanding given what she shared about her trauma. But after the countless late nights of intense and personal confessions, King realized that Syncere's affliction not only stemmed from the violation but her feelings of abandonment.

While he believed she trusted him, Syncere avoided defining their relationship. King wanted clarity - exclusivity. From his perspective, Syncere was only his - his partner, his princess, the woman he loved. King did not doubt that Syncere cared for him. They spent every available second together, and her level of public affection and intimacy increased every day, but he wasn't certain if it was love for her. The sparkling grey eyes from the picture on his phone pleasantly interrupted his daydream.

"Hi, Princess. I was just thinking about you." King smiled. "Is everything ok?"

"Hi, King. Yes, everything is fine. I just wanted to catch you before my appointment with Dr. Jacky. I know you have more meetings this afternoon."

"Baby, you know you can call me at any time." He paused, sensing something going with her. "Syncere, are you sure you're ok? Are you nervous about your appointment?" He questioned.

"Um - no - yes. I don't know. I just feel like I'm in a good place and Dr. Jacky wants to not only talk about Mariah, but she asked me to write a letter to my rapist." Syncere hadn't disclosed a name to King because she was convinced he would hunt him down wherever he was and kill him. "I know she's the professional but I don't see how this is beneficial."

"Princess, you have history with the doctor, right? Maybe she wants to push you further than you've gone in the past. If you trust her, then you have to trust her process."

"Yeah, I know you're right. I'm just - I don't know. I guess I'm scared." She admitted.

"Baby, I'm sorry I'm not with you right now." King deeply exhaled, checking his email to determine if his assistant was able to reschedule his afternoon so he could get to Syncere. "Write the letter from your heart - write it from your hurt, Syncere. Whatever and however you need to say it." He paused. "I'll be there soon, okay. Call me after your appointment. Please let me know you're ok."

"Okay, King. I miss you too by the way." She bashfully gleamed as they disconnected the call.

———

PEPPERMINT TEA and meditating to the sounds of the makeshift waterfall were becoming Syncere's weekly routine while she waited for Dr. Jacky. She'd already relinquished her cell phone to the receptionist and removed her shoes, but she was angst, unsettled. Writing the letter to Davis was brutal, but to read it aloud, devastating. And Syncere had not talked about Mariah since she revealed her truth to King. Giving her up for adoption was the one decision that Syncere was fairly settled about. Of course, she had moments of regret, but they quickly diminished once she observed the happiness in the sparkling grey nine-year-old eyes that matched hers.

"Well hello Syncere, my dear. Come on in." Dr. Jacky beckoned.

"Hi, Dr. Jacky. You're looking awfully pretty today." Syncere giggled. "Do you have a hot date, good doctor?"

"Maybe I do, maybe I don't." She winked. "Should I ask you the same question? Normally, you are comfortable and casual when you come to see me. But you look awfully cute in your sweater dress and boots."

"Maybe I do, maybe I don't," They cackled. "King has been gone all week so I've been looking like a bum. I decided to put some clothes on today."

"I like King for you." Dr. Jacky blurted. "You are different with him - vulnerable, unresistant. He makes you feel secure, my dear. Am I right?"

Syncere didn't attempt to conceal her smile. "Yeah, he does. It's like he's always a step ahead - knowing exactly what I need and when I need it. It's a new feeling for me, but it feels good."

"Does it feel like love, my dear?" Dr. Jacky peered over her glasses.

"I don't know. I've never felt love for a man. Other than my grandfather."

"But you know what love is, Syncere. How do you feel when you're with him? Just describe it - don't think, just feel." The good doctor instructed.

"I feel...safe, free, relaxed, powerful, cherished, adored, bashful, sexy. I miss him when he's gone. I get butterflies just anticipating his face." Syncere paused, dewy-eyed. "I don't want to imagine another day without him." She tearfully confessed.

"My dear, *that's* love." As Syncere's smile expanded, so did Dr. Jacky's. "Well, I can scratch that off of our list. Syncere loves King - check." She giggled, marking on the lined paper. "Now, let's transition. Did you write the letters?"

"Dr. Jacky, we were having so much fun. Now you want to ruin it." Syncere tried to deflect. "Yes. Yes, I wrote the letters."

"You choose which one to read first. Take a deep breath and start when you are ready." Dr. Jacky's voice soothed.

Syncere closed her eyes, inhaled then blew it out, inflating her cheeks. She unfolded the typed paper, chewing on her lip, tapping her foot. *Write it from your heart - write it from your hurt.* She meditated on King's words and calmed.

"Davis, you are a rapist. I know that I was not the first and unfortunately probably wasn't the last. You steal innocence, you steal joy with no care for anyone but yourself. You are a filthy despicable person for what you did to me. It pains me to know that I've lost so much time, so many opportunities to love, blaming myself because of your actions. Questioning, did I drink too much? Should I have dressed more conservatively? But none of that matters because

*it happened and you did it - **you raped me**. You violated my body, destroyed my spirit, and planted your undesired seed. But today Davis, I am stronger, better, wiser. Today, you will **no longer** have power over my life. Your scent will no longer haunt me. I refuse to allow the barriers I built because of you to continue to block my life. I will live, I will love. And you don't win."* Syncere deeply exhaled, expelling every ounce of her truth from her heart and hurt.

"Well done, my dear. Well done." Dr. Jacky silently clapped her hands together. "I'll see you next week."

Crinkled forehead and pouty lip, Syncere was puzzled. "I thought we were doing the letter for Davis and Mariah." She probed.

"Nope. You keep the letter to Mariah. Maybe one day you'll be ready to give it to her." Dr. Jacky winked and Syncere sighed in relief, clutching the handwritten letter to her chest.

———————

SYNCERE PULLED her Lexus into the parking lot of her building, ready to return to the office. She glanced at her phone, it was after 4 pm. Syncere walked around the corner to the front of the building, noticing a somewhat familiar car parked across the street in front of Nate's Barbershop. Walking into the office, Syncere was greeted by an unfamiliar face at the receptionist desk.

"Good afternoon, how can I help you?" The unknown receptionist greeted.

"Good afternoon. I'm Syncere James. I work here. May I ask who you are?" Her brow furrowed.

"I'm Toya from the temp agency. I'll be covering for Ms. Ella until Tuesday." She smiled.

"Oh yes. I completely forgot Ms. Ella and Justin were leaving town today. My apologies. Nice to meet you, Toya." Syncere extended to shake her hand. "Any messages for me?"

"You have a client waiting in your office and I forwarded a few emails from new clients requesting appointments with you," Toya confirmed.

"Thank you. Don't hesitate to let me know if you need anything Toya. I'll be here late so just lock the front door when you leave." Syncere walked to her office while texting King to let him know her appointment went well and she was back at the office. Syncere couldn't immediately determine who was sitting at her desk until she pushed the door open.

"What's up baby girl?" Lamont's dark muscly frame stood to greet her.

"Lamont. What are you doing here?" Syncere cautiously offered a one-arm side hug.

"That's not happiness to see me, baby girl." Lamont bantered.

"Lamont, we haven't talked in months. Why would I be happy to see you sitting in my office unannounced?" Syncere sat in her office chair, crossing her arms over her chest.

"You've been ghosting me Syncere. I thought we were friends. I've missed you, baby girl." Lamont sat at the edge of the guest chair with his elbows on her desk.

"Lamont, I wasn't ghosting you and we are friends. I've

had a hectic couple of months. A lot has changed in my life so don't take it personal." Syncere shrugged.

"So, can you get away tonight?" Lamont licked his lips. "Can we get reacquainted?"

"Nah, Lamont. It's not like that anymore." She coyly chuckled. "No more, um, agreements for me."

Lamont reached across the desk to caress her hand. "Syncere, are you trying to tell me you have a man now? And you didn't give me a chance?"

"A chance? Lamont, what are you talking about?" She hailed.

"Yeah, a chance, babygirl. Do you really think I've been hanging around for a year just for our agreement? I've always liked you Syncere. I was just waiting for you to be ready to shift our relationship." Lamont continued to rub his thumb across the palm of her hand.

"Lamont, I'm sorry. But - somebody else has my heart. You are amazing, but you-you're not the one." She timidly smiled.

"That Amistad dude, right?" Lamont chuckled.

"His name is King, but yeah, him." She blushed, placing her free hand on top of his. "Lamont I'm sorry—"

"Syncere? What is going on?" King angrily interjected, eyeing the handheld connection from the doorway.

"King!" She nervously paused, standing from the chair. "You remember Lamont?" Lamont stood to his full height, still shorter than King.

"It was good seeing you babygirl but let me get out of here." Lamont attempted to exit the office but King didn't move. "Excuse me, dawg."

"Syncere, what the fuck is going on? You got your fuckboy up in here. Are you serious right now?" King howled, still blocking Lamont's path.

"Fuckboy?" Lamont chuckled. "Man, it's not what you think, dawg." Lamont interposed.

"Dawg, I don't want to hear shit you gotta say, man." King stepped closer to Lamont. "You need to bounce - quickly."

"King. Please stop. Lamont just stopped by unexpectedly. Just let him leave so we can talk." King and Lamont continued their staredown. "King! Please!"

King leered at Syncere then back to Lamont before he exited her office, allowing Lamont to begin his departure.

"For what it's worth man, I just dropped by to say what's up to baby girl. She didn't know I was coming, dawg." Lamont followed behind King, attempting to offer an explanation.

"Dawg, back the fuck up. Like I said, I don't need to hear shit from you. Bounce." King was eerily calm, silently daring Lamont to take another step towards him.

"Lamont, please just go," Syncere begged. He obliged, exiting the office without taking a look back. She followed behind him to secure the office door. King gawked at her, anthracite orbs narrowed and frigid. "King. I can explain."

The office was empty. The temporary receptionist left and locked the front door as instructed. But King had a key, entering the office to surprise Syncere, not expecting to find her holding hands with another man.

"Explain what Syncere? How do you explain you smiling and holding hands with a nigga you was fucking? Not that long ago I might add. You think that nigga just wanted your fucked up agreement. He can get pussy anywhere. Nah, Princess, he wanted *you*." King shouted. "I knew that shit the first day I met him."

"King. I haven't talked to Lamont since right before we went to Brighton. And I haven't seen him since Melvin's. He just showed up here and the temp receptionist let him in my office." Syncere reached for King but he pulled away.

"So, everybody is to blame but you? Did you tell him about us?" King questioned.

"I told him that a lot has changed for me and that I was seeing somebody, yes." She muttered.

"Syncere!" He snapped. "Did you tell him that we were together? That I am *your man*, not another fucking agreement?" Syncere paused for a second too long. "I'll take that as no." The life was sucked from King's body. His distress and outrage were palpable. Syncere quaked as King's dewy-eyed intense gaze punctured her soul. He was hurt, motionless, defeated.

"Princess, I don't know what else to do. I've remained honest and truthful about my feelings since the beginning. Moving at your pace, at your time, in your control. But the fact that you can't make it crystal clear to that mutherfucker that we are together. That you can't say that *I'm* the one you want. That's problematic - a major issue for me." King dropped his head, shaking in disbelief.

"King, it's not how it appeared. I was trying to explain to Lamont what was going on. Telling him about you - about us. This is all new for me and it's just hard for me to explain."

"That can't always be your excuse, Syncere. You feel something. It shouldn't be that hard to explain." King paced the floor, rubbing the back of his neck, unsuccessfully quelling the tension.

"King, you know how I feel about you. It's not an excuse. It's difficult for me to be vulnerable, but I'm trying, King - I'm trying to remove the barriers." Syncere slowly minimized the distance between them. "King, you know you have my heart."

"But do you *love* me, Syncere? Because I am absolutely, unequivocally, *in love* with you, Princess. I think I always have been - since the first day we met. But your rules, walls, barriers, agreements, whatever you want to call them have denied you so much. You've been running, protecting yourself your entire life Syncere - from your mother, that mutherfucker who will die on sight if I ever find out who he is...and me."

"You? King, how have I been running from you?" She questioned.

"You've been running from me, from what we could be for eight months, Syncere. If after everything we've shared, everything you've trusted me with, you can't decide if you want to be with me, if you love me, Syncere.... Then...we just need to let it go." King footed across the office desperately needing to escape. His chocolate-covered skin was now flushed with pain. Syncere grabbed his corded arm, his pace halted, constantly weakened by her touch.

"I don't want to let it go, King. Babe, I -I don't want to let you go." Syncere whispered against his pulsing bicep.

"Then stop running, Princess." King cupped the curves of her face. "I promised you I will never hurt you. I'll always keep you safe. If you let me - as your man, Syncere. The man who loves you."

"King, I - I don't know how to do that. I've been running for so long... I don't know how to stop." She cried.

"Let me show you, Princess. Just let me love you."

King invaded her mouth slowly, yet firmly replicating a whisper, "Syncere, I love you. I always have." She wept softly into his sweet embrace as he caressed her earlobes, addictively conquering all of her senses. Their full lips and tongues enmeshed, tangled, hungry - the sensual taste test nearly buckled their knees. Syncere was completely adrift and disoriented by the depth of his words and the reliance of his eyes.

"I-I do love you, King. I just-"

"Shh." He paused her words. "No explanation needed. Just leave it at '*I love you.*'"

Syncere's grey eyes were thunderous, face stained with tears, she repeated her confession through a hushed whimper. King's tremendous frame backed them into her office, simultaneously devouring both sides of her neck, his hands caressing through her freshly styled, bobbed curly tresses. He closed the door and the blinds, concealing the moment, although the office was empty. King effortlessly rested her on the desk. Syncere trailed her fingers up his chest, pulling the branded Polo shirt over his head, using it as her personal handkerchief to dry the tears that continued to blur her vision.

Planting a soft kiss on his lips, Syncere navigated her way to his massive neck, inhaling the citrus and sandalwood cologne while she tickled the folds of his nape with her tongue. Rubbing her hands up his goosebump-covered chest, her tongue trailed down the same path, fondling his nipples until he flinched. "Shit, Princess." King adjusted her grey sweater dress, practically lifting her entire body off of the desk, disrobing her from the dark grey boy shorts.

Syncere unzipped his slacks, releasing the countless inches of heaviness that King possessed. He melted into her folds, immediately occupying residency within her plump, enticing, and saturated treasure. The curves of her body were engraved in his psyche, requiring no direction to gratifyingly thrust and pierce every corner and curve of her jewel. King's shirt that once dried her tears was now tightly cloaked around his waist, she tugged - begging, urging him into her depth.

For Syncere, every time felt like the first time with King as he found delightful, mind-blowing ways to satisfy her. Cupping her ass, he possessively nudged her to the edge of the desk, hoisting her legs towards the heavens, black Coach boots dangling in the air. He relentlessly plunged into her treasure, immersing deeper, harder, faster, she welcomed every painstakingly blissful lash of his girthy demand.

"King. Oh, my goodness. Baby. I can't-" Syncere moaned, back arched, head hanging between her shoulder blades, hands achingly gripping the corners of the desk.

"You can't what Princess? Tell me what you want." He whispered, still deliciously thrashing.

"King." She grunted.

"You want King, baby. Tell me Syncere." He slowed his pursuit, the tip of his shaft circling against her private lips, teasing her.

"Ah, shit, baby. I want you. King. Please." Syncere sexily screamed, informing all the neighbors of his name.

King released the animal, lustfully rekindling her lips, pleasingly pounding into her treasure until candied juices satiated the immeasurable circumference of his dick. Moments later, King experienced an intensely salacious release of his own.

"Fuck! Princess!" He groaned.

Syncere collapsed, weakened by his love and intimacy. King secured her, palming the small of her back while buried in the folds of her moist neck. Labored breathing, they glared at each other, harmoniously whispering, "I love you," lacking urgency to disconnect their sultry, tender, affectionate, nurturing embrace.

11

"Zeus, please stop drooling on me." Syncere chuckled as she opened one eye, viewing the cutest dog as the sun beamed through the floor to ceiling windows in King's master bedroom. She spent the week with him at his condo since he stayed with her the week prior. It had been two weeks since the Lamont fiasco and Syncere's confession of love for King. They'd been inseparable and relished every minute. She checked her phone to verify her schedule for the day, noticing a text from Symphony.

Prima: Hey Prima. I know you are still buried under Lion King so I didn't want to disturb you. It'll just be me at dinner tonight with G-ma. It's a long dumb ass story so don't ask. I'll pick you up around 5. Love you.

Syncere was definitely going to ask what happened when she saw her cousin, but for now, she just responded, *I love you too.* The cousins were taking G-ma to dinner, along with

King and Symphony's friend Calvin, but apparently, he was no longer joining.

"Zeus! Get off the bed. You know better, crazy dog." King entered the bedroom shirtless, looking tastefully tempting. Syncere alluringly smirked as he wriggled into the bed. "Good morning Princess." He kissed her navel, trailing down to her infinity tattoo. "Can you be late today?"

"King, if it was up to you, I would be late every day." She giggled as he continued to tickle. "Babe, I can't. I'm meeting with Justin to run through the marketing presentation for the client meeting tomorrow."

"Ok, Princess." He blushed, still tickling her navel with his tongue. "Are we still meeting at 6 pm tonight?"

"Yes, G-ma has been looking forward to getting out for dinner all week. She even had her hair and nails done yesterday. You have spoiled her already." Syncere lifted up in the bed, kissing his forehead before footing into the bathroom to start the shower.

"She's no more spoiled than you, Princess." He teased.

"Excuse me, sir? I don't remember ever getting a special delivery breakfast, lunch, and dinner with flowers." Syncere peeked out of the bathroom door, brushing her teeth.

"But you did get roses every day last week and a massage by *moi*." He proudly pointed to himself as if she could see.

I guess I am a little spoiled. Syncere giggled while cleansing her face, then reappeared in the bathroom doorway naked. "Hey, babe?" King raised an eyebrow, staring at her beautiful mahogany body. "Maybe I can be a little late." She crooked her finger, beckoning him to her.

Syncere and King showered together, making mad,

passionate love as if it was the first time. Syncere had made tremendous strides over the past few months, consistently seeing Dr. Jacky and surrendering to King, who treated her more like a queen than a princess. King was everything she secretly wanted, but never knew she needed to completely heal. A man who guarded her heart, stimulated her mind, impassioned her body, and was openly willing to protect his woman at all cost.

"Princess, coffee and breakfast are ready when you are." Leaning against the bedroom doorway, sexy as hell in a navy blue suit, King glared at her as she finished dressing. "You are absolutely beautiful. Seriously, you take my breath away. And don't tell me to stop." He winked.

Syncere finger-combed through her damp curly hair, dressed in layers to brave the crisp November air. King still made her nervous, embarrassed, she was certain he could see the goosebumps through her leopard print cardigan. She grabbed her Louis Vuitton Neverfull, bent to tickle Zeus' ears before padding over to King, following him into the kitchen made for a master chef. King pulled out her chair before taking his seat, then led them in prayer. They enjoyed bagels with veggie cream cheese, boiled eggs, and turkey sausage.

"Babe, is it too late to adjust the reservation for tonight?" Syncere questioned, taking a sip of the perfectly blended coffee.

"Um, I'm not sure, what's up?" King probed.

"Looks like old man river won't be joining Symphony tonight." She chuckled.

"That's so wrong, Princess. That man's name is Calvin." He paused. "How old is ole dude anyway?" King chuckled.

"Too old for Prima. I know that much." Syncere rolled her eyes, laughing, but irritated by the thought of her cousin dating a man twenty years her senior. "I definitely can't judge anyone for letting their personal issues impact their life, but - I just want to see her happy. Like she wanted for me."

"I know, Princess. Symphony is a smart, beautiful woman, she'll figure it out." He paused. "Maybe I can see if Tyus is available tonight. They connected in Brighton, so maybe she won't mind. What do you think?" King inquired.

"Hmm. Now you're trying to play matchmaker." She quipped. "But that may not be a bad idea. If nothing else, he can flirt with G-ma, at least she'll be happy."

"Baby, make sure you text her so it won't be a surprise. If she's anything like you, she doesn't like surprises." He joked.

They finished their breakfast, then left to start their day. King dropped off Syncere at the realty office before visiting a few construction sites then meetings in his office. He was constantly preoccupied with thoughts of Syncere as he stared at her picture on his desk. She was doing so well, no nightmares, but he worried about her when they were apart. Is she too stressed? Did she eat? He worried about anything that could trigger a panic attack and cause her to spiral.

King was a true alpha male, fiercely protective and some-what territorial. He wanted her with him 24/7. King loved waking up to her honey-glazed scent every morning after a night of exploring her bodacious frame and falling asleep wrapped in those mocha thighs. The mere thought of her thighs caused his mouth to water.

"Yo, King." Tyus knocked on the office door. "What's up, man? You look deep in thought."

"What's up, bro?" King shuddered, detaching from the visual of her thighs to focus on work. "You got some numbers for me?" Tyus was King's accountant but also had a law degree so he often reviewed new business contracts to ensure the financials were solid.

"Yes sir." Tyus took a seat at the desk across from King. "The contract looks good. You would profit quite nicely from this commercial deal. This project is small enough where it would not compete with your father's company since I know that was a concern." King's father owned Cartwright Construction, managing only commercial projects for the past 25 years.

"But?" King probed. "You look like you have more to say."

"You know me well, bro." Tyus paused. "My only concern is that this company, The D. Reed Group, needs this business badly. If this deal doesn't go through, they may be bankrupt." King's brows creased as Tyus continued. "Yeah, they've made some pretty risky investments over the years that fell through so they are banking on this contract with you and Davenport."

"That is a good piece of information to have in my back pocket for tomorrow's meeting. Thanks, Tyus, greatly appreciate it, man." King and Tyus dapped. "Hey Tyus, you have plans tonight?"

"Nah, TJ is with his mom this weekend, so I'm free. What's up? Don't tell me you're coming up for air from Syncere to kick it with yo boy." He quipped.

"Ha! I guess I deserved that. Princess has been my primary focus lately. But I ain't complaining. That woman can have all of my damn time." He mused, envisioning those mesmerizing grey eyes. "I'm taking Syncere and her grand-mother to dinner tonight."

"You want me to keep grams company, dawg? Is she as fine as her granddaughters?" He heartily guffawed.

"Nigga, you stupid as hell." King chortled. "Symphony is joining us so I thought maybe –" King's voice trailed off, hunching his shoulders.

"You thought I could occupy Symphony?" Tyus sat back in the chair. "Man, that girl is something else, dawg." He shook his head.

"Shit, if she's anything like her cousin, you ain't gotta tell me nothing." King chuckled. "What's up? What's the problem?"

"You know we kicked in Brighton, right. She was cool as hell. I reached out to her after we got back and she was acting funny like she didn't want to be bothered." Tyus paused, adjusting in his seat. "Then, she hit me up randomly one Saturday night. I think she was drinking, asking me to come through, but I had TJ. So, I told her that I got my son and she started questioning me about why I didn't tell her I had a son. Asking if I was married. How was I supposed to tell her anything personal when we ain't talked? And we damn sure didn't do a whole lotta talking in Brighton, if you know what I mean..."

"So, I take that as a no. You don't want to go to dinner." King shrugged while laughing.

"You know what, dawg. I'm going to go. I want to see how she acts." Tyus agreed. "But don't tell her I'm coming."

"You crazy as hell. You ain't fucking up my night. My shit

is guaranteed to go down unless Syncere is mad because Symphony is mad." King explained.

"Nah, dawg. I promise you, it'll be cool. Trust me." Tyus guaranteed. King nodded in agreement.

———————————

SYMPHONY PICKED up Syncere at the realty office. Syncere was standing outside talking to Deeny and Nia from the salon when Symphony pulled up in her black Audi A5 coupe.

"What's up bitches?" She rolled her window down, shouting.

"Hey, girl." Deeny and Nia responded. "I love the new car," Nia commented.

"Thanks, girl. Prima, let's go. You know G-ma is waiting in the lobby with her coat on and scarf around her head." Symphony stressed.

"I'm coming," Syncere said her goodbyes as she opened the passenger door. "I knew I should've driven my car. Now I have to be crammed in your little ass back seat when G-ma gets in." She whined.

"Just hush and come on. Such a baby. Everybody doesn't have a Lion King to chauffeur them around." Symphony teased.

"Whatever heffa. He doesn't chauffeur me around." Syncere focused on her phone, informing King that they were on their way.

"Whatever bitch! When's the last time you drove your car

anywhere, Syncere?" Symphony's brow raised, leaning over to hear the answer.

Syncere whispered. "Two weeks."

Symphony shouted. "What was that?" She laughed.

"Ok, two weeks." Syncere joined the guffaw.

"I rest my case," Symphony affirmed as she pulled in front of the assisted living building. G-ma was indeed in the lobby waiting.

"Well don't you look pretty?" Syncere boasted as G-ma smiled. The aides helped her grandmother into the car and put the wheelchair in the trunk. Symphony expressed the same sentiment.

"Ok! I see you G-ma with your red lipstick to match your scarf." Symphony squealed.

"G-ma, I think you're trying to steal my man," Syncere exclaimed from the backseat.

"Girly girl, I've already had the love of my life. I don't need yours." G-ma confidently expressed.

"Who said King is the love of my life?" Syncere questioned, shifting to get comfortable in the back seat.

"G-ma, should I start or you got this one?" Symphony quipped.

"Oh, I got this one girly girl." G-ma cackled. "Why is King the love of your life? Let's start with that glow you've been wearing or the permanent smile on your face. Maybe it's the way you look at him. Or the way you run to get your phone when he calls or eagerly respond to his text like you just did."

"Or maybe it's the butterflies in your stomach that will start to flutter right about....now because there he is."

Symphony heartily teased, pulling up to the restaurant valet as Syncere beamed at the sight of King.

"Who is that man with him?" G-ma probed. "They are two towers of fine." She was tickled.

"Oh shit. I mean, shoot. Sorry, G-ma." Syncere paused. "Prima, I completely forgot that King invited Tyus." Symphony rolled her eyes at her cousin, knowing she was lying before turning her gaze to Tyus. She was speechless, fingers locked to the steering wheel, recalling how his velvety lips felt against her skin.

"Prima, let me out. My legs are falling asleep." Syncere shouted.

Symphony was still mute, popping the trunk as Tyus rounded the car, staring at her. He got the wheelchair from the trunk while King opened the passenger door.

"Well, hello, lovely lady. It's great to see you again, Mrs. James." King kissed G-ma's cheek, then helped her into the wheelchair. "Mrs. James, this is my friend Tyus Okoro." G-ma was beaming ear to ear, being cared for by two gorgeous gigantic men.

It was pretty frigid outside so they hurried into the restaurant where they were seated in a private room. The surrounding glass doors offered privacy, yet visibility into the crowded restaurant. King didn't miss the opportunity to embrace Syncere, pulling her into a forehead kiss.

"Hi, pretty lady. I missed you today." He smiled.

"I missed you too, babe." Syncere reciprocated, taking the seat he pulled out for her.

"What's up Symphony? How have you been?" Tyus spoke, signaling her to be seated. Symphony was fruitlessly ignoring him, however, the blush across her cheeks was evident to everyone but her.

"Hi, Tyus. I've been good." She cracked an imitation smile.

Syncere leaned over, gritting through her teeth. "Prima, what is your problem with Tyus? Your attitude is nasty. Don't ruin G-ma's night." She demanded.

"Whatever. But I hear you and I understand." Symphony excused herself from the table, heading to the restroom. Syncere would make sure she got some answers from her cousin later.

The waitress brought drinks and appetizers as King and Tyus attentively listened to G-ma share how she met her husband, Mr. James, while the cousins reminisced about their grandfather.

"Ms. Neolla, how long were you married to Mr. James?" King questioned.

"I met Mylon James when I was 17 and he was 20. I was a senior in high school, waitressing at Melvin's to help momma with the bills. Mylon was home on leave from the Air Force. He was tall, dark, and handsome, and I was a looker back then - much like my girls." G-ma winked at Syncere and Symphony.

"Mylon watched me all night without saying a word. He would smile and wink at me before I even knew his name. I got off late that night, and there he was, waiting to walk me home. My Mylon was a quiet man. After introducing himself, he held my hand and walked me all the way home in silence, stealing glimpses of each other and blushing." G-ma reminisced. "But I knew he would be my husband - and he was for 51 years."

Although Syncere heard this story several times, she was enamored by her grandparents' love story. She reminisced about how attentive, protective, caring her grandfather was to his wife, granddaughters - and even his daughters, although the relationship was tainted. Before Davis, Syncere dreamed about that type of love story - an intense, affectionate, devoted, unconditional kind of love. Syncere unconsciously brightened as she gazed at King, ruminating if he was the love of her life - if they could love each other for the next 50 years.

"What was it about that quiet walk home? How did you know he would be your husband?" King heedfully inquired, focused on her every word.

"You know King, he made me feel safe, protected, secure - without many words. Mylon didn't need to say a lot because he showed me a lot. And that's how he demonstrated his love for 51 years." G-ma smiled, dewy-eyed.

"I always love that story G-ma. Poppa could just give you a look, and you knew exactly what he was thinking and needed." Symphony chimed.

"And he did the same for me. It's called *love*, girly girl." G-ma chuckled. "You girls should try it sometime." She winked.

King was staring at Syncere, internalizing every expression of devotion G-ma spoke. He loved Syncere unconditionally, ready and willing to protect her at all costs.

They savored the rest of their dinner; laughing and talking. Even Symphony and Tyus were amiable, a glimpse of the flirtatiousness resurfaced. G-ma thoroughly enjoyed herself, especially the strawberry cheesecake.

Exiting the restaurant they contined their cheerful banter

as they waited for the cars. Tyus said his goodbyes and hopped in his Mercedes, pulling behind Symphony's car since he offered to follow her to G-ma's. Syncere kissed her grandmother through the car window and narrowly eyeballed Symphony, silently threatening her to be nice to Tyus. King was patiently waiting for Syncere at the passenger door of his SUV. She hopped in, but not before kissing him.

"THANK YOU, KING," Syncere whispered against his face.

"For what Princess?" He questioned.

"For being so nice to my grandmother. She had a ball tonight." She giggled.

"Baby it was my pleasure." He gazed before securing her seatbelt and closing the door. They momentarily rode in silence during the 20-minute drive to his condo.

"Princess, I adore your grandmother. She is just a breath of fresh air. I would've loved to meet your grandfather." He smiled, caressing her palm with his thumb.

"Poppa was an amazing man. I remember when my mother showed up drunk one day. I was maybe ten or eleven. Me and G-ma were crying, begging her not to take me with her. Poppa pulled up in his truck, walked over to my mother taking me from her grasp, instructing me to go into the house. I watched from the window as my mother cursed and yelled, claiming she wanted to see me. Poppa's demeanor didn't shift, simply told her to leave - so calm it was scary. She left and that was the first time I saw him cry." Syncere reminisced, heavy eyes fixed on nothing. "He always protected me - all of us."

"I want that to be my responsibility, Syncere." King stayed focused on the road. "To protect you, make you feel safe."

"You do make me feel safe, babe." Syncere nervously grinned.

"Princess, I mean I want to protect you for the next 50 years like your Poppa protected your G-ma. I want that Mylon and Neolla type of love - with you, babe." He smiled broadly.

"King. Stop." She paused, peering at him, fully aware of her dismissive behavior. "I-I don't want to have this conversation. Not tonight."

"Syncere don't do that." He glowered. King despised when she instructed him to basically stop loving her - stop feeling the way he felt.

"Do what, King?" She questioned.

"Telling me to stop - stop complimenting you, stop expressing my feelings, shit, stop loving you. I won't stop that shit Syncere. So you need to stop instructing me to do so." He paused, trying to choose his words carefully because he was pissed. "But I don't understand why can't we ever talk about our relationship? You never want to talk about what's next for us. You're on cruise control while I'm ready to accelerate." King pulled into the garage, turned off the truck but didn't move. "I feel like we are at an impasse, Princess. And - it scares the shit out of me."

"King, babe. I just don't want to discuss it right now. We're in a good place and I want to keep it that way. Right?" Syncere queasily probed.

The ache in King's eyes made her feel sick. He exited the truck, rounding to the passenger side to open it - hushed, quiet. King and Syncere walked into his house greeted by Zeus' barking. King removed her coat, hung it in the closet, and footed across the great room to the bedroom, still inaudible. He was irritated, frustrated - pissed. Syncere eyeballed King as he disappeared into the dusky hallway. *Shit!* Syncere slapped her palm against her forehead; she knew she'd fucked up - again.

12

King never required an alarm to wake up in the morning. He was always up before the sun, and in the past few weeks, he would awaken to the most captivating hum of Syncere's light snore. King could lay for hours into the morning, gazing, fascinated by her silky chestnut flesh, hypnotized by the rise and fall of her abundant breasts. He stretched his arms, prepared for the most exhilarating embrace, but the bed was empty. King jolted, peering around the expansive bedroom searching for his princess. She was gone.

King was annoyed with Syncere last night, taking a shower and retiring to bed without further conversation about their relationship. But that didn't change his craving for her morning caress. *Is she sick? Did she have a panic attack? Did she leave?* He pondered every sane and insane scenario. King rolled out of bed, footing to the dresser to get a pair of shorts since he was naked. He switched on the bathroom light checking for her - it was empty.

5:48 am. He glanced at the clock on the wall before leaving his bedroom, padding down the hallway into the dimmed living room. King continued his exploration, locating her perched on the chaise lounge facing the patio doors.

"Princess," King whispered. "Are you ok?" He slowly meandered towards her, careful not to startle just in case she was having an attack.

"Yes and no." Syncere slightly smiled, grey orbs reddened.

"Baby, did you have a nightmare?" King knelt beside her, thumbing a tear from her face.

"No. Nothing like that." Syncere cupped his face, locking eyes so that he was assured she wasn't having an episode. "I was just thinking about Mariah." She handed King an envelope addressed to her from a Mr. and Mrs. Alvin Malloy.

Syncere checked her mail before she left the office yesterday and received a letter from Mariah's parents. She dropped it in her purse, not really considering it until she got settled last night.

"She's learning how to tap dance and loves to sing," Syncere whispered as King opened the envelope to find an invitation to the Briar Woods Elementary School's Fall Festival scheduled for that day at 5 pm.

"How long have you had this? This invite is for today." King questioned.

"I haven't really been home, King." She smirked. "I just checked my mail yesterday."

"What do you want to do, Syncere?" He placed a hand against her jolting knee.

"I desperately want to meet her, but I don't know if I can do it, King. What if she asks me about him?" Syncere softly cried.

"Princess, maybe just seeing her is the first step. Then if you feel like you're ready to actually meet her face-to-face, you can." King joined her on the chaise, cuddling behind her. "But only if you're ready babe. You know I'll go with you if you want. Whatever you need."

"Thank you, babe. I appreciate you so much, King." Syncere shared a sweet kiss. "I'm sorry I frightened you. I was just tussling in the bed and didn't want to wake you, but Zeus has been keeping me company." They both peered down at the sleeping dog, curled up like a baby.

"Ha. Some company he is." King laughed. "Baby, you should try to get a little more sleep. You need to be rested for your presentation today - and whatever you decide about seeing Mariah."

"Nah, I'm up now. If I go back to sleep, y'all may not see me at the presentation." She chuckled. "I think I'm going to take a swim in your bathtub."

"Okay. You get your bath started and I'll make you some peppermint tea. Bet?" King bantered.

"Bet. Thank you, King." Syncere wrapped her arms around his bare waist, resting against his chest for a minute longer than planned, inhaling his aromatic morning scent. "I love you, King and I'm sorry about last night." She detached from him, no eye contact as she ambled into the bedroom.

King was immobile, still breathless, eyeing Syncere until

she disappeared from his sight. That was only the second time she'd verbalized her love for him in that way. King wasn't shy about saying 'I love you' to Syncere verbally or in a text. Her typical response though was: 'me too babe,' 'I appreciate you,' or a heart emoji - never mouthing the words since the night they made love in her office. Syncere's voluntary expression of affection and apology was the motivation King desired to progress their relationship further.

Syncere savored in the steamy jacuzzi tub, enjoying a cup of peppermint tea. Mariah still occupied the forefront of her mind, but she had to focus on her presentation. This new contract could be lucrative for Davenport Realty and she didn't want to be the reason they lost the business. Syncere practiced her talking points as she got dressed, deciding to leave early so that she could drop by the office before conducting two house showings, before the partner meeting at 3 pm.

"Princess, are you sure you don't need me to drive you to the office?" King stood at the double bathroom sink mirror fixing his tie while Syncere applied her makeup.

"Babe, it doesn't make sense for you to drive to Haven this early just to come back in this direction for your meeting. I can drive, King. I promise you, I'm fine." She assured him.

King walked Syncere to her car, hesitant about her driving after the emotional morning. They passionately exchanged an embrace before separating. King observed her as she pulled out of the driveway. He understood that Syncere was a strong, powerful woman, but he was distressed to see her in anguish about possibly seeing

Mariah. King wanted to protect her from anything that caused her emotional or physical suffering.

Syncere called Symphony while driving to the office, being her morning alarm for a change.

"Hey, Prima. You're up early." Symphony sleepily laughed.

"Today is that partner meeting I was telling you about. I'm going into the office a little early to get prepared." She paused. "But you know that's not why I'm calling. What was your problem last night?"

"Girl, I just thought Tyus was somebody that he's not." Symphony sighed.

"How Prima? Y'all was mighty tight at the lakehouse. What happened?" Syncere interrogated.

"He has a son." She paused as if Syncere was supposed to react. "Tyus never mentioned a son the entire weekend in Brighton." She yelped.

"Okay. He has a son...and?" Syncere was confused.

"You know I don't do ex-wife or baby momma drama. I don't have time for that kinda foolishness." Symphony rolled her eyes.

"Ok Symphony. I am not doing this with you today because what you just said is silly. You don't know that man - aside from whatever went down at the lakehouse - and you don't know his son's mother." Syncere was irritated, reflecting on how her cousin scolded her about giving King a chance.

"But Prima—" Symphony tried.

"Nope. Not doing it. Bye Prima." Syncere interrupted, clicking the end call button on her steering wheel.

TODAY WAS NOT the day for Syncere to have two talkative clients who still didn't make a decision. She dashed into the office with about fifteen minutes to spare after the two house showings ran late. "Hi, Ms. Ella," Syncere shouted as she kept trotting to her office. "Bye Ms. Ella." They chuckled.

"Syncere, everything is all set. Your copies are already in the conference room." Ms. Ella echoed as Syncere continued to scamper through the space.

She stopped by the restroom, tidied up her hair and makeup, reviewed the high waist black slacks that shaped her curves and red button-down top, before returning to her desk. She deeply exhaled, calming her nerves. Syncere was confident in her abilities, but the stakes were high, so she was nervous. Her phone chimed, indicating a text message.

King: Hi Princess. Are you here? We are wrapping up the contract review. You are going to kill it, babe. I'm here and I love you.

Justin's voice blared through the office phone speaker, indicating that the group was ready for her. Syncere text a red heart emoji back to King. She pondered for a second, thinking back to last night, deciding to stop playing games and let the man know how she truly felt. Syncere sent a second text message, *I love you too, King.*

Syncere grabbed her portfolio and glass of water, confidently strolling towards the conference room. She lightly knocked, hearing Justin's voice inviting her in, opening the door, she immediately connected with King's therapeutic eyes across the room.

"Hey Syn. Come on in. We are looking forward to your presentation." Justin stood, signaling her to sit between him and King on the opposite side of the table from the client. Syncere rounded the twelve seat conference table, prepared to greet the new business partners. Justin continued. "Davis Dubois, this is our top sales agent and marketing manager Sync—"

"Syncere James." Davis interrupted, reaching across the table to shake her hand, but she recoiled, motionless. "After all of these years, you still look good enough to eat." He smugly smiled.

Syncere's breathing was labored, heaving, debilitated by his nightmarish timbre, familiar stench of cologne, and the dangerously crude smirk.

"You two know each other?" Justin and King inquired almost in unison.

"Oh yeah. I know Syncere." Davis licked his lips, an egotistical grin across his demonized face. "How have you been, sweetness?"

Still tongueless, Syncere felt like she was being smothered, her hands trembled, dropping the glass of water. She quivered at the crashing sound, peering down, eyeing the shattered pieces of glass scattered across the dampened conference table. Syncere released everything from her hold and sprinted out of the room, heart pounding, threatening to damage her ribcage.

Justin and King wore matching scowls, confused by what just happened while Davis leisurely sat in his chair, turning to his business partner uttering, "She was always a feisty one."

King's eyes narrowed, gawking at Davis, geared to jump across the table to snatch that smug attitude and insensitive comment off his lips. Clearly, something was troubling Syncere, and King was going to get some answers. He darted out of the room, calling her name, checking her office when Ms. Ella directed him to the restroom. King gently pushed the door, certain it would be locked but it wasn't. He opened the door, verifying that she was alone. Syncere was hunched over, pressed against the wall, hyperventilating, gasping for her next breath. King placed his hand on her back, bending to connect with her eyes.

"Syncere, baby, what's wrong? What is going on?" King questioned. "And don't tell me you're fine."

Still panting, Syncere regarded him, frightened, terrified. "Dav-. Dav-." She was suffocating, wailing, screaming with fear. "It's Dav-" She uttered. King glared, nudging her chin to bind with her leaden grey eyes. Searching them for under-standing, discovery. Syncere peered back at him, praying that he would comprehend her distress without words. King pondered, recognizing the same expression of terror, trepida-tion, and disquietude she wore the day of her panic attack. The breathless mumbling, *Dav-, Dav-,* he recollected hearing while she slept on the patio at the lakehouse. King's eyes narrowed, breathing intensified, he was *irate* at the real-ization.

"It's *him*." King angrily whispered, already knowing the answer.

"Yes." Syncere breathed, nodding profusely, clutching her chest.

Internally, King was infuriated, ready to release his

wrath, but he had to remain calm for Syncere. "Baby, I need you to breathe. Please Syncere." He massaged her back, kissing against her forehead until her panic attack began to settle. Justin knocked on the door.

"Hey. Is everything ok in there?" Justin questioned, peeking into the restroom.

"I - I'm okay. I'm so sorry, Justin. I'm fine." Syncere stood upright, inhaling and exhaling deeply, steadying her gasping.

"Princess, are you sure you're okay?" King probed. Syncere locked with his eyes then nodded, and instantaneously, King bolted past Justin, leaving the restroom. Syncere knew that King was heading towards Davis. "Justin, stop him. King will kill Davis." Still confused, Justin followed her directive.

King thrashed into the conference room, dragging Davis from his chair, weighty hands clenching his neck.

"Man, what the fuck is your problem?" Davis choked through his words, feet practically dangling in the air.

"You are my fucking problem. Tell them what you did?" King's grip tightened. "I swear to God I will kill you, dawg. Tell them what you did to her?"

"Did - did to who?" Davis struggled.

"King! Let him go." Justin shouted. "What the hell is going on, man?"

"Nah, Justin. This mutherfucker has something to say before I let his ass live. Tell them what you did to Syncere." King's obsidian healing eyes were now coal-black and vacant; he'd snapped.

"I ain't do shit to her." Davis carefully exhaled.

"You raped me!" Syncere shouted from the doorway. "The

Davis Reed Dubois raped me ten years ago." She moved into the room, eyes focused on Davis, but she ensured his business partners comprehended every word. "He lured me to his apartment, locked me in the room. Davis slapped and choked me. He raped me." The thunderous wail and vehement pain were palpable. "I had to leave school because *of you*. My friends, my life - all of that changed because *of you*. I isolated myself for two years with nightmares, panic attacks, migraines - you stole *everything* from me."

"This bitch is lying. Everything that happened she wanted." Davis yelled as King yanked him off of the wall by his collar, just to slam him back into the wall with two mammoth hands clenching his neck. Davis fought to breathe.

"Say another mutherfucking word. I swear to God, I will put your ass to sleep." King was eerily calm, which was dangerous - at least for Davis.

"You can say anything you want to Davis, but I know what happened. I remember the resounding shriek of my screams; I remember clearly saying *no*. But you will no longer haunt me, you will no longer have control over me. I will live, I will love. And your life will be miserable, Davis. You won't ever win." Syncere's calmness matched King's repose as she impassively left the conference room.

Gathering her purse from her office, Syncere realized what just happened. She'd confronted her rapist who was still in the next room gasping for air because of her boyfriend's chokehold. Her mood quickly shifted from calm to frenzied, hurriedly exiting the office through the back door, running to her car. The Lexus' tires screeched out of the parking lot, speeding down Main Street.

King hadn't relinquished Davis' neck. He was not exaggerating about murdering that nigga on sight, but Justin convinced him that Davis wasn't worth his freedom, attempting to pry King's tightly clutched fingers from Davis' neck.

"King. King. Stop it!" Ms. Ella yelled. "Syncere just ran out of her and sped off down the street. I'm worried about her King. Stop it now." Ms. Ella's screams quaked King from his rage.

"Today is your lucky day, but if you even think about Syncere James, I *will* kill you." King dangerously leered. "Oh, and Justin, count me out. I don't do business with slimy mutherfuckers." King released Davis' neck, dropping him like a ragdoll.

"Oh, no worries, King. Davenport Realty will not be doing business with the D. Reed Group." Justin ensured as he turned his focus to Davis. "Get the fuck up out of my office, dawg."

King rushed to his truck parked in front of the building. He called Syncere, receiving her voice mail. He tried again and sent a text message with no response. ***Princess, please pick up the phone. Baby, where are you?*** King mused.

13

S yncere pushed the red button to decline the call for at least the 20th time since she'd bolted out of the office. She hadn't seen or heard about Davis Dubois since that fateful night ten years ago, often wondering what she would do - how she would respond if Davis crossed her path. Although Syncere was still visibly shivering at the sight of Davis, a slight smile developed across her mouth, proud of how she handled the situation. The blaring of the phone rang through the car's speakers again. It was King. *I can't talk to him right now.* She mused, whispering aloud. "Baby, I'm sorry."

Syncere only had the capacity to focus on one thing at a time and right now, she had to pay attention to the road, viewing through burning, red, clouded eyes. She was certain that King was worried sick, but she would call him once she arrived at her destination.

King was distressed, concerned about Syncere, given the

afternoon's tumultuous events. He had no dream that she would face her rapist and it would be a potential business partner. King had met Davis once in Chicago during the early stages of the contract negotiations, but Syncere never disclosed the identity of her violator. They didn't discuss the prospective business since she was not involved until a couple of weeks ago. King wished Syncere would've given a name, so he could have prevented this day from happening. He had to find her; he needed to observe those majestic grey orbs to confirm that she was unharmed, mentally and physically. *Come on Princess, pick up the phone.*

King wasn't sure where she could be. He called Syncere, drove by his house, and searched for her car at G-ma's assistant living building. Nothing. King continued to drive, hoping that his next stop would yield results. If something happened to her while he was wasting time choking the shit out of Davis instead of running after her, he would never forgive himself. King left another voicemail message.

"Princess, please pick up the phone. Baby, I need to know that you're ok. I've looked everywhere. Syncere, please. I love you so much and I don't know what I would do if...babe please, just call me."

After driving 45 minutes outside of Haven Point, Syncere pulled into a parking lot, eyes closed, head leaning against the black leather headrest. She pushed the voicemail button to listen to King's messages, each one ending with a sentiment of love. Syncere desperately desired to have him near her. While she demonstrated more power than she ever thought she could under the circumstance, Syncere needed King's strength and stability. She needed to hear him call her his princess. Syncere text him to ease his concern, *King, I'm ok. I promise I will call you soon. I love you too babe.*

Syncere exited the silver Lexus, peering at her red stiletto heels, wishing she would've grabbed her flats from the office. She gingerly footed across the parking lot, opening the vast steel door of the fairly new modern building. The click of her stilettos against the tile floor muffled the sounds and visuals from earlier that played on repeat in her psyche. Syncere followed the sounds of people and music down the long hallway. The multihued paper sign that read, *Fall Festival*, hung above the wooden double doors to an auditorium. It was a little after 5 pm and the place was already crowded with proud parents and family members obstructing views with their cellphones in the air to capture the moment their child graced the stage.

Syncere stood in the back of the auditorium, not bothering to find a seat because she honestly was uncertain if she was going to stay. She leaned against the wall, anxious, fidgeting, second-guessing her decision to attend. Syncere checked her phone, seeing no response from King. She dropped the phone in her tote, glancing around the auditorium while two 3rd grade brothers performed a clumsy juggling act. Syncere checked her watch, seriously contemplating leaving - she felt she'd made a mistake, but she waited for the next performer's name to be called.

"Hi, Princess." King's soothing intonation welled tears in her eyes. He placed his hand on the small of her back, eliminating the distance. "Baby, are you okay?"

King's warm breath against her face was the tenderness she coveted. "Yes, I'm okay." She nodded, leaning her back into his chest, head resting on his shoulder, finding relief in his caress.

"Our next performer will be singing Whitney Houston's "*The Greatest Love of All*". Please welcome, Mariah Syncere Malloy." The festival host blared through the microphone.

Syncere inhaled deeply, anticipating the sight of her daughter for the first time aside from pictures. The purple satin dress and black patent leather shoes came into view before Mariah did.

Syncere gasped, covering her mouth with both hands as tears streamed down her face. The stunningly pretty little girl rendered her breathless - identical grey orbs, curly shoulder-length hair, styled with a purple ribbon to match her dress, hazelnut satiny skin, and an angelic voice.

"Princess, she's beautiful." King tightened his embrace as he whispered. "Just like her mom."

"Oh my God. I can't believe it's her. She is so pretty. She's amazing." Syncere cried.

Mariah sang her heart out, then joined her class to sing the Black National Anthem as Syncere joined the brigade of families proudly recording their children. Syncere simply admired her from afar, pondering how similar they are. She felt like she was viewing a mirror - seeing herself at nine years old. Syncere mouthed a silent prayer of thankfulness that Mariah's life was happy and full.

She noticed two people standing in admiration of Mariah as well, cheering their support. *Her parents*. She smiled, their faces were simply glowing with pride.

"I'm ready to go." Syncere turned to King, suppressing the thunderous tears. He surveyed her, reading her eyes.

"Ok. Let's go, Princess." King didn't need words to understand. He escorted her down the hallway. "Baby, ride with me. I don't want you driving. You're exhausted."

"King, I can't leave my car here. I'll be fine." She uttered, lips quivering.

"No, you won't. I'll take care of your car. Syncere, do you trust me?" Although he requested, King wasn't taking no for an answer.

"Always," Syncere whispered.

King opened his passenger door, ensuring she was secure. Syncere reclined in the seat, staring out of the window, finally discharging the trapped tears. The ride was silent and Syncere was asleep in less than 30 minutes.

———————

ABOUT AN HOUR LATER, the white Escalade pulled into the driveway. Syncere was in a deep sleep, not moving when King closed the car door. He walked around the truck and opened the passenger door, nudging her awake. Syncere shivered, awakened by the crisp chill of the night air. She blinked, attempting to focus her eyes, not immediately recognizing her location. Syncere lifted from the seat, rapidly blinking, the extravagant white frame house and black shutters became clear.

"King! Are we in Brighton?" Syncere's sleepy eyes quickly became wakeful.

"Yes, Princess, we are." King smiled.

"Babe. Why? What are we doing here?" She questioned.

"Syncere, can we discuss this inside? It's cold out here." King speedily ushered her to the front door, unlocking it and illuminating the house.

"King, why are we at your family's lake house? I thought you were taking me home - well, to your house."

"I did bring you to my house, Princess." He winked as he ambled further into the house.

"Now you have jokes. King, what is going on?"

"Baby, I just wanted to get you away from Haven for a little while. The school was only an hour from Brighton, so I contacted the housekeeper, Marna, once I realized where I could find you. She grabbed a few things for us to have tonight and made sure the heat was turned up." He paused. "Princess, you've had a traumatic day and I simply want you to rest."

Syncere contemplated objection but she acquiesced. She was exhausted and the lakehouse actually gave her joy. "Thank you, King. I don't know what else to say." She shrugged.

"Thank you will suffice, Princess." King kissed her forehead, leading her into the master bedroom. "Are you hungry?"

"No. I just want to sleep." Syncere stretched and yawned. "Don't try to make me eat, King."

"I'm not. Although I want you to eat something, I'm not going to press." King crossed his arms, leaning against the doorway watching her.

Syncere undressed as King disappeared into the kitchen. She washed her face, examining her reflection in the wooden framed mirror. She was conflicted. Syncere was sullen, dispirited, tremendously sad, yet relieved, solaced, extremely grateful.

Syncere footed across the bedroom draped in an ivory robe; pulling her hair into a ponytail, she crashed onto the bed requiring slumber.

"Princess, I brought you some tea." He whispered. "It's chamomile. I hope that's ok."

"Yes, babe. It's perfect. Thank you." Syncere reached for the cup, placing it on the nightstand. King gazed at her while she sipped the tea, digesting the depths of her eyes, seeing the struggle.

"Syncere, what do you need?" He questioned, still dressed in his suit, standing next to the bed, one hand stuffed in his pockets.

"I need you, King. That's all. That's it." King securely cradled against her, still fully clothed. He didn't care, he was what she wanted, needed, so he willingly obliged.

King roused from his sleep around 2 am, missing Syncere absent from his embrace. She'd shifted to the edge of the bed as she often did when she was deeply hibernating. *I love that sound.* He meditated on the hypnotic purr of her slumber. King was still dressed in his suit pants and shirt, deciding to take a shower so that he could quickly return to her.

The colossal granite shower offered six temperature-controlled body massage jets and a rain shower head. King turned up the heat as hot as he could stand it, allowing the jets and showerhead to massage his muscled physique. King leaned a hand against the steamed tile wall, reflecting on the craziness of yesterday. "I really could've killed him." He mused, recalling the moment when he snapped, prepared to murder Davis and contentedly suffer the consequences. Syncere had him willing to kill for her, that's how much King loved and adored his princess, but was her heart fully accessible? Favorably inclined to demolish her barriers and grant him full access? He hoped, prayed that she was, otherwise he believed he wouldn't recuperate from the wretchedness.

Syncere lengthened her arm, stretching to regain King's caress, but the space was unoccupied. She rose, searching the room, observing the light peeking from under the bathroom door. Syncere was still in her robe since they didn't have clothes. She tip-toed across the chilled hardwood floor, softly knocking on the slightly cracked door. Syncere caught a glimpse of King's sinfully exquisite dark chocolate naked skin, immediately flooding her treasure.

"You ok, Princess?" King opened the bathroom door, dick dangling.

"I am now." She blushed, licking her lips, making no attempt not to stare at the curve of his beautiful dick. "I needed you, but you were gone."

"I'm right here. What can I do for you, pretty lady?" He bit his bottom lip, disrobing her with his eyes. "What do you need Syncere?"

Closing the distance between them, Syncere didn't say a word, just motioned her pointer finger, directing him to come closer. King happily obliged, lowering his head to her for easy access.

Syncere softly drew a line with her tongue across his brawny neck while simultaneously stroking his titanic stiffness. King flinched, his swollen veins pulsating against the palm of her hands. Kissing one earlobe before journeying back across his neck to inhale the other lobe, Syncere whispered, "Baby, I need you." Without ceasing her relentless stroke, Syncere tongue-kissed down his chest, circling her toasty tongue around his muscle-bound pecs.

"Shit, Princess. What are you trying to do to me?" He moaned, knees weakened, still standing at the bathroom threshold. King trailed a single finger down the opening of her robe. Slowly, he tugged the loosely tied belt, letting the robe drop slightly to expose the rise and fall of her perfectly rotund breasts.

They tangled in a passionate push and pull as they simultaneously encouraged one another into the bedroom. Still soft, gentle, and sensual as fuck, King won the battle, forcing her body to walk backward. Syncere took control, turning around to grab his hand, expediting the remaining distance to the king-size bed.

"Siri, play Lauryn Hill's *The Sweetest Thing*," King uttered to activate the music.

Syncere was still standing as King reclaimed the folds of her neck, aimlessly mapping her body, nibbling and caressing all of his favorite locations. He tugged at the loosely fitted robe, letting it fall at her feet while he beheld the allurement of her body.

"You are so fucking beautiful, Syncere," King grunted, possessively capturing the curves of her face. He sauntered around her to sit on the bed, positioning Syncere between his legs as he continued his surveillance of her frame - ready to execute on his plan.

King and Syncere had experienced all facets of love-making - soft, sensual, raw, and rough but he knew exactly what she needed today. To be made love to, passionately, delicately.

"Princess, I love you so much. Do you understand that?" He intently proclaimed.

"Yes. I understand, King." She whispered.

"Tonight, I just want you to relax and let me give you everything you need. Whatever you want, baby, I got you." He sexily smiled. "Bet?"

"Bet." Syncere blushed.

King tongue - kissed around her belly button, paying close attention to his favorite tattoo. Syncere's legs weakened, literally buckling in his embrace. King seized her, effortlessly placing her on the plush bed. He continued his pursuit, gently licking her scar before journeying to her treasure. His warm breath, teasing, pleasing - her candied nectar bubbling over. Syncere was completely delirious, eyes closed tight, unable to find words in anticipation of the pleasurable attack King was certain to deliver.

King needed to see her smokey grey orbs, even if he was about to make them roll into the back of her head. "Princess, open your eyes."

With heavy lids, Syncere opened her eyes to witness his buttery chocolate skin licking his lips like he was about to feast. And that's exactly what he did. King stayed swimming in her juices for what seemed like a lifetime - she bucked and gyrated her hips to his salacious rhythm. King literally sucked the life out of Syncere. She slightly passed out but was coherent enough to feel King's gentle kisses on every bead of sweat and quiver, placing his final sweet nectar-filled kiss on her cheek whispering, "Sweet dreams, Princess. I love you."

14

It was *11 am.* Syncere gazed at the digital clock with one eye opened. She felt intoxicated, hungover, but she was certain the only libation she had last night was King. Curly chestnut brown hair was scattered across the pillow as Syncere negotiated a release time with the mattress that was holding her hostage. She didn't need to reach for King to know that he was no longer in the bed. "This man can't stay in the bed past 8 am." She spoke softly to nobody but herself. Syncere reached for her phone confident that King messaged her his location - he always did. *Getting us a few things. I'll be back shortly sleepyhead.* She blushed.

Finally winning the battle with the bed, Syncere meandered to the bathroom, turning on the jetted shower that King raved about. The rain shower and the jet combination had her in a trance, completely forgetting that she didn't have hair products to revive her curly tresses. After getting good and saturated, Syncere reluctantly departed the shower, wrapping her hair in a towel and re-dressing in the robe, figuring it would be her attire for the weekend.

Walking out of the bathroom, Syncere noticed a red tote bag on the bed that wasn't there before. Her brow creased, wondering what was in the bag as she approached the bed. The tote revealed a bra, panties, leggings, shirts, socks, a pair of flats, Crest Whitening toothpaste, Olay lotion, Dove deodorant, and Shea Moisture Curl Enhancing Smoothie. Syncere beamed, overwhelmed by King's attentiveness. He knew exactly what she needed.

Since the day he brought her the perfectly crafted coffee to the office, King proved that he wanted to provide her with absolutely everything she desired - known and unknown.

"Hey, Princess." King's bass-filled tone caused a gratifying shudder. "Do you have everything you need?"

Syncere studied his words, trying to quell the mist generating in her eyes. She was so thankful and appreciative of a man like King, although her behavior sometimes said otherwise. "Yeah, babe. I have absolutely everything I could ever need right here."

"Um, good. I'm glad." King stuttered, comprehending the depth of her statement. "I brought food. You really need to eat Syncere."

"Ok. Ok. Let me get dressed." She smiled until he disappeared.

Syncere ambled into the living room, soaking in the view of the lake before she found King sitting at the kitchen island with his laptop.

"Baby, you're killing it in your Target gear." King chortled.

"Don't hate on Target. This outfit is too cute. You did

good, Mr. Cartwright." Syncere teased. "I see you chose grey sweatpants, out of all the options in Target."

"What?" He peered down at his clothes. "What's wrong with grey sweatpants?"

"Nothing. Nevermind babe." Syncere blushed, admiring the fullness of his thighs - among other things in those pants. "What's for lunch?"

"I grabbed a little surprise." He grinned, pulling a container from a brown paper bag. "A chicken bacon ranch panini and French onion soup from Touissant's," King recalled Syncere lauding over her meal during brunch at the winery several weeks ago.

"OMG! King, that is seriously the best -"

"Soup and sandwich you've ever had." He completed her sentence. "I know babe, you bragged about it the whole ride home from Brighton."

"Whatever! The only thing that would make this surprise a ten is –"

"A bottle of Touissant's red blend wine," King interjected again, finishing her thought.

"How do you think of everything?" Syncere was in shock and awe.

"That's easy. Because it's for you, Princess." King candidly proclaimed as he opened the bottle of wine. Syncere grabbed plates and bowls from the cabinet to unpackage their lunch, still unclear about how and why he was so perfect.

"Let's eat on the patio," King suggested, interrupting her daydream.

"Babe, it's cold outside. We can see the lake from the dining room table." Syncere pouted.

"Princess, the screened-in part of the patio is heated." He smiled. "I'll grab the food, you get the wine."

They footed over to the heated patio wearing their Target best. Syncere and King delighted in the food, wine, the view of the lake, and each other's company. They laughed, talked, daydreamed silently for a couple of hours on the patio. They'd transitioned from the patio dining table to the over-sized chair facing the lake.

"Have you talked to Justin?" Syncere questioned, tangled in King's embrace.

"Yeah, earlier today. He called to check on you." King replied, nestled against her face.

"I have to figure out a way to fix things." She deeply exhaled, pondering the craziness with Davis and its impact on the business contract.

"Fix what, baby?" He queried.

"The contract. Make sure you all can secure the business. I know how profitable it would be for you and Justin." She paused. "I need to figure out a way to make it work - partnering with Davis' company."

King sprang up, shifting Syncere with him. "Syncere, do you really think we would go into business with that mutherfucker?" His eyes were eerily reminiscent of yesterday when he choked Davis. "I don't give a damn how profitable it could be."

"King, I understand that sometimes things are just business, not personal." She shrugged.

"Syncere look at me." She didn't move. "Baby, look at me." He snapped. "When it comes to you, it will *always* be personal for me. And Justin thinks of you as his sister, so I'm sure it's personal for him too. Business ain't that damn important. If you thought I was going to sit across from Davis trying to conduct business, knowing what he did to you -" King couldn't finish his statement, just thinking about what Syncere endured infuriated him. "Besides, he needed our business more than we needed him."

"What do you mean?" Syncere probed, forehead creased.

"Before I enter any new business deals, I have Tyus investigate the prospective company. The D. Reed Group is facing bankruptcy. They - he needed our business to stay afloat." King shrugged. "Karma is a bitch, ain't it?" He laughed.

"She's a big ole stanky ass bitch, and I love her in this case." Syncere heartily guffawed. "I think I just shocked myself yesterday. I never thought I would be able to face him, but I realize I am much stronger than what I thought. But I really just did what you told me to do."

"What's that?" He inquired.

"I spoke from my heart and my hurt." She smiled, connecting with his healing orbs.

"Princess, I've always seen and admired your strength. You are a boss, baby." He fingered a loose tendril falling across her face. "You spoke your truth yesterday, so there shouldn't be any regrets." King paused, contemplating if he should probe about a specific statement she made during her rage. He decided to articulate what was on his heart. "You also said that you will live and - love. Was that a part of your truth from your heart?"

"Yes, King. It's absolutely a part of my truth. While the physical wounds healed quickly, there were pieces of me that were shattered, irreparable. And now - I feel like my soul is anchored and my heart is healing. It's still a process, but I feel a shift and I'm not scared anymore."

"Scared of what? Him?" King probed.

"No. I'm not scared to let my heartbreak or heal, or just simply let my heart - love." Syncere modestly smiled, but the twinkle in her eyes proudly gleamed.

The couple continued their lovingly lazy Saturday on the patio - talking, laughing, drinking, snacking, lovemaking - repeat. This fiery, impassioned behavior sustained until they fell asleep bound, affectionately intertwined.

SURPRISINGLY, Syncere was the first to awaken still cuddled on the patio. She didn't disjoin from King, just simply nestled in the rise and fall of his comforting chest. Syncere peered at him, admiring his chiseled, yet gentle face, sexily framed by his well-groomed beard. She ran a finger across King's Hershey chocolate lips, continuing to trace down his neck, tickling his Adam's apple. She tenderly kissed him there.

"Are you trying to start something, Princess?" King smiled, eyes still closed. "I rebound fast, but not that damn fast, baby."

"You're so silly. No babe, I rarely wake before you. I just wanted to look at you." She grinned.

"And what do you see?" King narrowly opened his eyes, gazing directly at her.

"I see this fine specimen of dark chocolate." She giggled.

"Seriously Princess. What do you see in me?" King probed.

Syncere paused, recognizing the gravity of his inquiry. "I see you, King. I see a man who loves me unconditionally." With tears welled in the corners of her eyes, she continued. "I - I see my first true love."

King was elated. His smile emitted so much happiness, he didn't know what to do with himself. "Let's go to the lake." He unconsciously blurted.

"Huh? Say what now? Um, it's cold as hell, King." Syncere shouted.

"It's not that bad. We can light the fire pit and I'll keep you warm." He pouted. "Please, baby, for me. We won't stay long. I promise."

"If I get sick, you will be nursing me back to health. Bet?" She demanded.

"Bet." He agreed with a fist bump.

Syncere quickly realized that King's recommendation was not so unconscious after all. He'd planned this little outing by the lake, buying hats, gloves, scarves, and thermal socks during his Target run. King grabbed a few blankets out of the closet while Syncere filled two thermoses with whiskey-spiked hot apple cider.

They exited out of the patio door, down the steps to the trail leading to the lake. Tonight supplied another full moon emblazoned over the chilled lake. They sat on a two-seat chair positioned in front of the fire pit. King ignited the fire, adding more logs to ensure it heated quickly. King and Syncere cuddled in silence, reminiscing on their first night at the lake. The place where their relationship began to transform from friends to lovers. Syncere confessing her complicated layers and King committing to love her through it all.

"I remember that night at the lake. I wanted to dissipate everything that was plaguing you, although I didn't know the extent of your pain then, I knew that hurt and sadness resided deeply within you. And I wanted to take it all away, Princess. I wanted to protect you." King continued to stare at the lake. "I've always known Syncere."

"You've known what, King?" She whispered through a shiver, sipping the spiked drink.

"That you were my one. My princess, my queen. The love of my life." He paused, finally making eye contact with her. "I knew the day Justin introduced me to you. Those damn eyes - God, they had me in a trance." He glared at her. "I told Justin that I wanted you to myself, and he told me to fall back. *My lil sis is delicate*, he said. *Take your time*, he advised." King chuckled as he mocked Justin's voice. "So, I did. The more we became friends, the more I wanted you, needed you as my...everything."

King cupped her chin, warming her frosted cheeks with his gloved hands, encouraging her to look at him. He caressed her shaky hands and gazed into her mesmerizing grey orbs that were wide, glossy, and nervous. "I have something for you, Princess."

Syncere was frozen, not only because of the frigid temperature, but the sincerity, adoration, and emotions of his words. She loudly swallowed, exhaled, and tried to calm her nerves. King revealed a black velvet box - a little too big to be a ring box, which quelled some of Syncere's anxiety. He handed her the box, but she hesitantly stared between King and the box.

"Baby, please open it," King whispered, smiling coyly.

Syncere pulled the red ribbon, then opened the velvet box finding a silver bracelet adorned with diamond-encrusted charms - butterfly wings, sun, cross, infinity symbol, the letters S and M, and something that appeared to be out of place, too big for the bracelet.

"Princess, I love you with everything in me. This bracelet represents all of the things that you love and the things I love about you. But this ring - " King pulled the bracelet from the box, revealing the out of place item - a 3-carat princess cut ring dangling from the bracelet. Syncere gasped, covering her entire face with her gloved hands as she wept.

"Princess. Syncere, baby look at me." He whispered, gently prying her fingers away exposing her tear-filled face. "I bought this ring the day after you told me you loved me, Princess. That's all I needed to hear to know I wanted to spend the rest of my life with you. I've been eager to ask you to be my wife since then, but I know that you're not ready and you don't have the capacity to consider it right now - and that's ok." King assured, brushing a finger down her frosty nose.

"So, I'm not rushing you to make a decision. I promised you and your grandmother that I would not push you, go at your pace. So, I bought the bracelet as a placeholder for the ring - a daily reminder of what I desire of you when you're ready. If it takes weeks, months, years, the ring *and me,* Syncere, we'll always be here, on your time." King thumbed the tears from her face, kissing her trembling lips.

Syncere's beautifully majestic face was flooded with thunderous tears. She regarded his breathtakingly handsome face, the generosity of his heart, and the unconditional love that exuded from his soul. Syncere had wasted enough time building barriers and constructing noncommitments with inconsequential people. She was prepared to listen, hear, and understand her heart.

"What if I'm ready now?" Syncere uttered through a lulling weep. King's expression immediately brightened but was cautious. "King, you are my first love. My one true love. The only man in my life that I've cherished and adored. Aside from my grandfather, the only man I've ever trusted." She deeply exhaled as King brushed away the tears, enclasping her in his endearing embrace. Syncere reciprocated his steadfast, enthusiastic caress.

"King, I can't begin to comprehend my life, my world without you in it. So, if removing this ring from the bracelet means that I get to spend the rest of my days loving you as your friend, lover - your wife, then I'm ready. Baby, I'm so ready." Syncere massaged the curves of King's face, his healing eyes offered warmth and assurance. "King, baby, I love you so much. I just want to discard the shattered pieces and let you love me, at *our* pace, in *our* time."

EPILOGUE

"You ready to pay me that $500, King?" Nicolas patted King on the back.

"$500 for what, man?" King questioned, fixing his bowtie in the full-length mirror.

"Dawg, I told you a summer wedding at the winery was in your future - and now here we are." Nicolas guffawed, peering around the beautifully decorated parlor room, admiring himself in a blue Tom Ford suit.

"Indeed, you did, Nic. And here we are." King chuckled, tugging at the sleeve of his tan Tom Ford suit, complemented by an ivory shirt and bow tie. "Man, I will give you a million dollars as long as the bet ends with me marrying Syncere."

It was a beautiful Saturday evening in June at the Toussaint Family Winery. The brilliant red and orange sunset emblazoned the sky as hues of blue and pale yellow lighted the white gazebo overlooking the vineyard. Seventy-five of

Syncere and King's closest family and friends occupied the space, awaiting the bride and groom.

Seven months ago, King and Syncere perched by the frigid, still lake in Brighton Falls and declared their love for each other. Today, they were going to be husband and wife at the place that sealed their relationship.

"Oh my God. I think I'm going to throw up." Symphony squealed, dramatically clasping her stomach.

"Why are you going to be sick, Prima? I'm the one getting married." Syncere rolled her eyes.

"Exactly! You'll be all married and in love and shit. What about me?" Symphony pouted.

"I don't recall this being about you, drama queen." Syncere's friend, sorority sister, and bridesmaid Aminah said, joining Syncere's eye roll. Aminah Loveless was Syncere and Symphony's friend from college. She was an author and creative writing professor at their alma mater Monroe University. Aminah came to town to stand as a bridesmaid for her best friend.

"Syncere, are you ok?" Aminah inquired. "You actually look a little squeamish, unlike Symphony." She leered, shaking her head at Symphony's antics.

"I'm fine. Just a little nervous. I just need a mint or something." Syncere sighed.

"Ladies, it's time." King's older sister, Kieryn 'Kiki' Cartwright, peeked inside the larger of the two beautifully decorated parlors. "Oh, my goodness. Sis-in-love, you're gorgeous. My little big brother is definitely going to cry."

Syncere was stunning in an ivory satin off the shoulder mermaid gown with a pearl and crystal beaded waist that perfectly complimented her curvy shape. The sparkling cathedral train framed her pretty face, offering the perfect view of the glimmering grey orbs King loved.

"Thank you, Kiki." Syncere smiled. "Don't you start - you'll make me cry. This makeup is too flawless to mess up now."

"Yeah, Lion King is going to cry - and grab that ass." Symphony yelped.

"Watch your language, Symphony Monique!" G-ma demanded as Kiki wheeled her into the parlor room. She was lovely in a light blue chiffon dress and loose salt-and-pepper curls draping her shoulders.

"Syncere. My goodness, you are beautiful." G-ma sighed, trying to halt her tears. "Are you ready to go get that man, girly girl?'

"Yes ma'am!" Syncere declared.

SYMPHONY AND AMINAH sauntered through the double doors greeted by smiling guests seated in gold Chiavari chairs leading to the massive white gazebo adorned with yellow and white roses. Nicolas eyed Aminah from his position as best man; she was curiously familiar and devastatingly beautiful.

Tyus, on the other hand, unsuccessfully tempered his gasp once he caught a glimpse of Symphony in a pale yellow one shoulder floor length front-split chiffon dress. She temporarily tamed the big, curly afro for a smooth, straight ponytail. Symphony smiled brightly at familiar faces, capturing a wink from her boy toy Jameson before connecting with Tyus. *Damn!* She mused, surveying his strappingly manly frame standing as King's groomsman, reminiscing about the bend of his manhood that admittedly rendered her speechless. Symphony blushed at the thought of the flirtatious whirlwind with these two handsomely delicious men.

King patiently awaited to hear what Syncere called, *the perfect song* for her to walk down the aisle. The melodic sounds of Jennifer Hudson's *"Giving Myself"* filled the summertime air.

I never been who I wanted to be. I never felt completely free.

No one's ever had all of me. Or made me feel so beautiful and sexy.

Now I'm flying like an airplane. Now I'm riding on the open range.

Now I'm living out my destiny. I know the truth, I got it all in you and me.

I'm giving myself over to you. Body and soul.

I'm giving it all. I'm giving myself over to you now.

King reflected on the words, clearing his throat, venturing to suppress the haze forming against his orbs. He clearly understood the song's message - Syncere was ready to fully and completely give herself over to King.

The French doors opened, revealing his princess, and King audibly heaved, moonstruck by her beauty. Justin graciously escorted Syncere. He was the most logical choice to relinquish her to King's care, given their brother-sister relationship and his partial responsibility for this union. Since the day King laid eyes on her, he couldn't deny Syncere's allure and grace, but today, she was stunning, radiant, breathtaking - and King was breathless. *Princess.* He mouthed as she meandered towards him, they locked in an impenetrable gaze. With every step she made, King's obsidian eyes welled with tears. He was marrying his princess.

"Who gives this woman to be married to this man?" The minister's deep tone broke their trance.

G-ma, Symphony, and Justin said in unison. "We do."

King eagerly stepped off of the platform to collect Syncere. The thunderous tears were no longer a threat. King's tears released months of anticipation, hopefulness, yearning, and adoration that occupied his heart. Syncere dabbed away his tears with her grandmother's silk handkerchief while vainly restraining her own. King escorted her up to the platform as she handed the red and yellow rose bouquet to her maid of honor Symphony, then interlocked hands and eyes with her future husband.

"We are gathered here today to celebrate one of life's greatest moments, the joining of two hearts and souls. We are blessed to witness the joining of Syncere Monae James and King Elias Cartwright in marriage. For them, the routine of ordinary life has delivered the extraordinary. They met each other, developed a friendship, fell in love, and are finalizing their love in the eyes of God and you as witnesses." Reverend Marx proclaimed. "King and Syncere, you have decided to write your own vows. Share them from your hearts." He declared.

Syncere smiled, preparing to share her vows. "King, I remember you advising me to speak from my heart and my hurt. But today, I am not only speaking from my heart, I am speaking from my healing. I told you I was complicated - well that hasn't changed much." She giggled to quell the tears. "But your healing eyes restored my wounded heart, stimulated new horizons and loved me as I was. King, you love me in ways I never knew possible - even when I'm being stubborn and hardheaded." They chuckled as King nodded his head in agreement.

"How blessed am I to be able to call you mine, my King, my first and only true love. You've been my rock, my protector, through my greatest challenges. You've encouraged me to grow and stay strong. In your arms and by your side, I am capable of anything. I love you, King. I prayed that God would order my steps and he led me to you, my husband." Syncere's voice quivered through tears. "I praise Him today as His will is being fulfilled. I will always love you my sweet King and rejoice in your love for me, at our pace, in our time, forever."

"My, my, my. I want to see you top that, son." Reverend Marx chuckled, nodding to King to begin.

"I'm definitely going to try my best." King exhaled. "Americano, four Splenda, four Sugars in the Raw, vanilla and caramel flavor, heavy cream blended. I heard the sweetest sound, rattling off the most complicated coffee order I'd ever heard." The crowd laughed, some very familiar with Syncere's coffee requirements. "I had no clue that minutes later I would be introduced to that sweet voice during a meeting at Davenport Realty. Those eyes - those damn mesmerizing grey eyes. They had me at hello. I knew the very first moment I saw you that we were meant to be together - you were supposed to be my Princess. Justin told me to pause - back up off of his play sister. But I couldn't stop because my heart knew. You have become my best friend, companion, lover, and life partner. Syncere, I love you with my whole heart, with a fervor and passion that can only be expressed in sugary kisses, gentle glances, and a tender caress."

King paused, examining her eyes, thankful that her painful past was no more. "Princess, I vow to always keep you safe, protect you from harm, be a shoulder to lean on when life is too much to bear on your own. I prayed for you, Syncere, and God led me to you, my wife." King's voice now matched Syncere's quiver. "I praise Him today and every day as His will is being fulfilled. I will always love you Syncere, my Princess, my love, and rejoice in your love for me, at our pace, in our time, forever."

"Well family and friends, I think we have just witnessed God's great work right before our eyes. What wonderful expressions of respect, honor, and love." Reverend Marx proceeded with the ceremony. King and Syncere never disjoining other than to light the unity candle and present their families with gifts. "I now pronounce you husband and wife. You may salute your bride."

Reverend Marx couldn't complete his declaration before King possessively captured Syncere's face, pulling her into the most passionate and alluring kiss. They lounged in that kiss for a lifetime and didn't care who was observing. King finally released Syncere, turning them to the crowd to be celebrated. They sauntered down the aisle, showered with cheers and well-wishes from their family and friends. Exiting through the double doors, they were whisked off to a private room to have some time alone while their guests enjoyed hors d'oeuvres and wine before the reception.

"MRS. CARTWRIGHT, I love you so much." King kissed against Syncere's forehead.

"I really like the sound of that - Syncere Cartwright." She giggled, melting into his embrace.

"Baby, I have something for you." King caressed the small of her back, leading them to the plush lounge chairs. He pulled out a gift bag that was stored in a drawer in the room. "This is for you, Mrs. Cartwright." He beamed.

"King, what have you done?" Syncere blushed. "Babe, the beautiful necklace you gave me for the ceremony and now this. It's too much-" King placed a finger on her lips, hushing her words.

"Open it, Princess." He ordered. Syncere pulled out a black box and opened it revealing a silver key and scroll of paper.

"A key and a piece of paper?" She curiously questioned.

"Yes, a key. Now open the paper." He instructed.

Syncere opened the paper, reading the fine print she

mouthed. *1913 Paramount Place, owners King and Syncere Cartwright.*

"King!" Syncere shouted. "It's a house! In Haven!" She practically tackled King, covering his chocolate-dipped face in kisses. Syncere was overjoyed to stay in her neighborhood since King was previously hesitant to move to Haven Point but granted his princess whatever made her happy.

"Yes, Princess, a house in Haven. It will be ready in about five months. You'll still be able to pick everything - I promise." Syncere parted his lips with her tongue, lovingly, intensely kissing him. King was ready to rip the expensive satin fabric from her body.

"Syncere... If we don't get out of here, I am going to consummate this marriage on this damn couch." King struggled to speak through her devotedly passionate kiss.

"Ok, ok babe. I'm sorry." Syncere panted as she tried to compose her simmering treasure. "Actually, I have something for you too." She sexily grinned.

"What have *you* done, Mrs. Cartwright?" King observed as she pulled a familiar black box from a different drawer. "Are you giving me the charm bracelet back?" He quipped.

"No silly. Just open it." Syncere nervously encouraged. King slowly opened the box, revealing the same charm bracelet that he gifted Syncere the night of their engagement. King's brow furrowed, confused, as he perused the charms one-by-one, trying to understand why she re-gifted the bracelet. *Butterfly wings, a sun, a cross, infinity symbol, the letters S and M, the wedding ring charm for her birthday, and -*"

King examined two tiny charms, then stared at his wife with misty eyes. "Syncere, is this a pacifier and baby shoes?"

King anxiously questioned as Syncere's grey orbs flooded with tears. "Princess, are you - are we having a baby?"

Syncere briskly nodded, shaking the tears from her eyes. "Yes, King. I-I'm pregnant, babe." Her voice nervily quivered. "Eight weeks, but I just found out on Thursday. I-I didn't want to tell you over the phone while you were in Chicago." Syncere was tense, concerned, scared that King didn't want a baby so soon after getting married.

"Baby, what's wrong? What are you not telling me?" King queried.

"Nothing. Nothing is wrong." She coyly smiled but it didn't brighten her eyes.

"Why do you look like you're afraid? Syncere your tone doesn't sound like you are happy. You are happy about this right, Princess?" King probed, caressing the curves of his wife's beautiful face.

"Yes, babe, I'm very happy. But - but are you? Happy? This is so much all at once, King." She stuttered.

"Syncere Monae Cartwright, aside from marrying you, nothing will make me happier than a pretty baby girl with her mother's mesmerizing eyes or a handsome baby boy as fine as his daddy."

King brightened, gently placing his hand against her beaded, sparkling waistband. "I love you, Princess." He softly kissed her lips, then bent down to whisper at her stomach. "And I love you too little munchkin." Recapturing her eyes, King lovingly reassured, directing his fist towards hers. "We got this baby. Bet?"

"Bet." Syncere's smile brightened the room. "I love you too King. And thank you, babe." Syncere sighed, just as Kiki softly knocked on the door, ready for them to enter the reception space.

"You're thanking me for what baby?" King dried her tears with the handkerchief while Syncere applied fresh lip gloss, readying themselves to be announced at the reception.

"For giving me another chance - a new opportunity at this." Syncere motioned to her concealed belly. "A chance to love."

THE END. THANK YOU.

LOVE NOTE TO MY READERS

Hey Loves! Thank you so much for reading Pretty Shattered Soul. I cried, screamed, laughed, and celebrated while writing this novel. Syncere and King were complex, nuanced characters that took me on an emotional roller coaster. I hope you felt every twist and turn and fell in love with them as much as I did! *Let me and the world know what you think by leaving a review.*

But what about our girl Symphony? Will her past pain and current private struggle dictate her future opportunity to find love? Who is she ready to love? Old man river Calvin, lil young tender Jameson, or half of the sexy twin towers Tyus? Stay tuned for Symphony James's story in Pretty Shattered Heart.

Get acquainted with the Haven Point neighborhood in my novella, French Kiss Christmas.

Follow me on Facebook and Instagram @LoveNotesbyRobbi-Renee, on Twitter @LoveRobbi.

Join the Love Notes private group on Facebook.

Shop all things Love Notes by Robbi Renee at www.lovenotesbyrobbirenee.com.

MEET ROBBI RENEE

Hey Loves! I grew up in St. Louis, Missouri (in the words of Nelly, "I'm from the Lou and I'm proud!) with incredible parents and two amazing older sisters. Being the baby of the bunch, I always had a vivid imagination and was wise beyond my years - *to grown for my own good* if you ask my mother! My love for talking too much, journaling, various genres of movies, books, and all things Oprah led me to complete a journalism degree, doing everything but being a journalist. I dishonored my childhood dreams of being in some form of entertainment, pursuing every career but anything related to reading, writing, or journalism.

I rekindled my love for reading and writing during the 2020 pandemic where my alter ego, Robbi Renee was born, starting my company, Love Notes by Robbi Renee. I was challenged to write and publish my first novella, *French Kiss Christmas*, published December 2020.

Robbi Renee draws upon personal experiences with life and love. My written works are inspired by my adoration for Black love, and stories of romance, heartache, trauma, intuition, and redemption.

Stacey/Robbi Renee enjoys her own Black family love story with her husband and teenage son. Don't miss what's next for Robbi Renee at www.lovenotesbyrobbirenee.com

Made in the USA
Columbia, SC
29 July 2024

b630d8bb-504d-4eca-a776-06ba2cea7793R01